"Married?" Faith interrupted Nash in a shocked voice. "No! We can't! That's not possible."

"I'm afraid it isn't merely possible, Faith, it's essential. You and I have to get married. We don't have any other option."

"Why?" she asked Nash, her voice high with defensive panic. "We don't—"

"Do you really need to ask me that?" Nash cut across her with grim cynicism. "Had you been more…experienced…"

"You're saying we have to marry because I was a virgin?" Faith demanded, disbelief coloring her voice. "But that's…that's archaic, Nash."

"To you I dare say it is, but it is the right thing, the only thing I can do now."

"And if I refuse?" she asked him, holding her head high.

"I can't allow you to do that."

RED HOT REVENGE

There are times in a man's life...

When only seduction will settle old scores!

Pick up our exciting new series of revenge-filled romances—they're recommended and red-hot!

Coming soon:

Cole Cameron's Revenge (#2223)
by Sandra Marton
On sale January 2002

Penny Jordan

THE MARRIAGE DEMAND

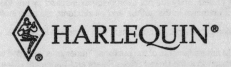

HARLEQUIN®

TORONTO • NEW YORK • LONDON
AMSTERDAM • PARIS • SYDNEY • HAMBURG
STOCKHOLM • ATHENS • TOKYO • MILAN • MADRID
PRAGUE • WARSAW • BUDAPEST • AUCKLAND

ISBN 0-373-12211-X

THE MARRIAGE DEMAND

First North American Publication 2001.

CHAPTER ONE

'DID you really think I wouldn't recognise you?'

The ice-cold darts of numbing, mind-blitzing shock pierced Faith's emotions as she stood staring in horrified nauseous disbelief. *Nash!* How could he be *here*? Wasn't he supposed to be living in America, running the multi-billion-pound empire she had read in the financial press he had built up? But, no, he was quite definitely here, all six foot-odd male animal danger of him: the man who had haunted her nightmares both sleeping and waking for the last decade; the man who...

'Faith, you haven't met our benefactor yet, have you?'

Their *what*? So far as Faith had understood, the huge Edwardian mansion so belovedly familiar to her had been handed over to the charity she worked for by the trustees of the estate that owned it. If she had thought—guessed—*suspected*—for one single moment that Nash... Somehow she managed to repress the shudder tearing through her and threatening to completely destroy her professionalism.

The Ferndown Foundation, begun originally by her boss Robert Ferndown's late grandfather, provided respite homes for children and their parents who were living in situations of financial hardship.

The Foundation owned homes in several different parts of the country, and the moment Faith had seen their advertisement for a qualified architect to work directly under the Chief Executive she had desperately wanted to get the job. Her own background made her empathise immediately and very intensely with the plight of children living in hardship...

She tensed as she heard Nash speaking.

'Faith and I already know one another.'

A huge wave of anger and fear swamped Faith as she listened, dreading what he might be going to say and knowing that he was enjoying what she was feeling, relishing it, almost gloating over the potential pleasure of hurting her, damaging her. And yet this was a man who, according to Robert, had, along with the other trustees of the estate, deeded the property as an outright gift to their charity—an act of such generosity that Faith could scarcely believe it had come from Nash.

She could feel Robert looking at her, no doubt waiting for her to respond to Nash's comment. But it wasn't Robert's attentive smiling silence that was reducing her to a fear-drenched bundle of raw nerve-endings and anxiety. Grittily she reminded herself of everything she had endured and survived, of what she had achieved and how much she owed to the wonderful people who had supported her.

One of those people had been her late mother and the other... As she looked around the study she could almost see the familiar face of the man who had been such an inspiration to her, and she could almost see too… She closed her eyes as she was flooded with pain and guilt, then opened them but refused to look at Nash; she could almost feel him willing her to turn round and make herself vulnerable to his hostility.

'It was a long time ago,' she told Robert huskily, 'over ten years.'

She could feel her fear sliding sickly through her veins like venom, rendering her incapable of doing anything to protect herself as she waited for the first blow to fall.

She knew Robert had been disappointed by her hesitation and reluctance when he had told her that he was giving her full control of the conversion of Hatton House.

'It's absolutely ideal for our purposes,' he had enthused. 'Three floors, large grounds, a stable block that can be converted alongside the main house.'

Of course there had been no way she could tell him the real reason for her reluctance, and now there would be no need—no doubt Nash would tell him for her.

The sharp ring of Robert's mobile phone cut through her thoughts. As he answered the call he smiled warmly at her.

Robert had made no secret of his interest in her, and had made sure that she was included as his partner at several semi-social events he had to attend as the charity's spokesperson. But so far their relationship was strictly non-sexual, and had not even progressed to the point where they had had a proper date. But Faith knew that that was only a matter of time—or at least it had been.

'I'm sorry,' Robert apologised as he ended his call. 'I'm going to have to go straight back to London. There's a problem with the Smethwick House conversion. But I'm sure that Nash, here, will look after you, Faith, and show you over the house. I doubt I'll be able to get back here tonight, but I should be able to make it tomorrow.'

He was gone before Faith could protest, leaving her alone with Nash.

'What's wrong?' Nash demanded harshly. 'Or can I guess? Guilt can't be an easy bedmate to live with—although you seem to have found it easy enough—and just as easy to sleep with Ferndown, by the looks of it. But then morals were never something you cared much about, were they, Faith?'

Faith didn't know which of her emotions was the stronger, her anger or her pain. Instinctively she wanted to defend herself, to refute Nash's hateful accusations, but she knew from experience what a pointless exercise that would be. In the end all she could manage to say to him was a shaky, proud, 'I don't have anything to feel guilty about.'

She knew immediately she'd said the wrong thing. The look he gave her could have split stone.

'You might have been able to convince a juvenile court of that, Faith, but I'm afraid I'm nowhere as easy to deceive. And they do say, don't they, that a criminal—a murderer—always returns to the scene of their crime?'

Faith sucked in a sharp breath full of shock and anguish. She could feel her scalp beneath the length of her honey-streaked thick mane of hair beginning to prickle with anxiety. When she had first come to Hatton Nash had teased her about her hair, believing at first that its honey-gold strands had been created by artifice rather than nature. A summer spent at Hatton had soon convinced him of his error. Her hair colouring, like her densely blue eyes, had been inherited from the Danish father she had never met, who had drowned whilst on honeymoon with her mother, trying to save the life of a young child.

Once she was old enough to consider such things, Faith had become convinced that the heart condition which had ultimately killed her mother had begun then, and that it had somehow been caused by her mother's grief at the loss of her young husband. Faith acknowledged that there was no scientific evidence to back up her feelings, but, as she had good and bitter cause to know, some things in life went beyond logic and science.

'What are you doing here?' she challenged Nash fiercely. No matter what he might believe, she was not—she *had* not—

Automatically she gave a tiny shake of her head as she tried to break free of the dangerous treadmill of her thoughts, and yet, despite her outward rejection of what she knew he was thinking, inwardly she was already being tormented by her memories. It was here, in this room, that she had first met Philip Hatton, Nash's godfather, and here too that she had last seen him as he lay slumped in his chair, semi-paralysed by the stroke which had ultimately led to his death.

Faith flinched visibly as the nightmare terror of her ten-year-old memories threatened to resurface and swamp her.

'You heard your boss.'

Faith froze as she listened to the deliberately challenging way in which Nash underlined the word 'boss'. Whilst she might have the self-control to stop herself from reacting verbally to Nash's taunt, there was nothing she could do to stop the instinctive and betraying reaction of her body, as her eyes darkened and shadowed with the pain of further remembrances.

At fifteen a girl was supposed to be too young to know the meaning of real love—wasn't she? Too young to suffer anything other than a painful adolescent crush to be gently laughed over in her adulthood.

'As a trustee of my late godfather's estate, it was my decision to gift Hatton to the Ferndown Foundation. After all, I know how beneficial it is for a child—from any background—to be in this kind of environment.'

He started to frown, looking away from Faith as he did so, the hard angry glaze she had been so aware of in his eyes fading to a rare shadowy uncertainty.

He had thought he was prepared for this moment, this meeting, that he would have himself and his reactions totally under control. But the shock of seeing the fifteen-year-old girl he still remembered so vividly transformed into the woman she had become—a woman it was obvious was very much admired and desired, by Robert Ferndown and no doubt many other gullible fools as well—was causing a reaction—a *feeling*—within him that was threatening the defences he had assured himself were impenetrable.

To have to admit, if only to himself, to suffering such an uncharacteristic attack of uncertainty irritated him, rasping against wounds he had believed were totally healed. He had, he knew, gained a reputation during the last decade, not just for being a formidable business opponent, but also for remaining resolutely unattached.

He closed his eyes momentarily as he fought against the anger flooding over him and drowning out rationality. He had waited a long time for this—for life, for fate, to deliver Faith into his hands. And now that it had…

He took a deep breath and asked softly, 'Did you *really* expect to get away with it, Faith? Did you really believe that Nemesis would not exact a fair and just payment from you?'

He gave a wolverine smile that was no smile at all but a cold, savage snarl of warning, reminding Faith of just how easily he could hurt her, tear into the fragile fabric of the life she had created for herself.

'Have you told Ferndown just *what* you are and

what you *did*?' he demanded savagely, causing Faith to drag air painfully into her lungs.

'No, of course you haven't.' Nash answered his own question, his voice full of biting contempt. 'If you had there's no way the Foundation would have employed you, despite Ferndown's obvious "admiration" for you. Did you sleep with him *before* he gave you the job, or did you make him wait until afterwards?'

The sound Faith made was more one of pain than shock—a tight, mewling, almost piteous cry—but Nash refused to respond to it.

'*Have* you told him?' he demanded.

Unable to lie, but unable to speak either, Faith shook her head. The triumph she could see in Nash's eyes confirmed every single one of her growing fears.

Giving her another of those feral, intimidating smiles that made her shake in her shoes but made her equally determined that she was not going to give in to his manipulative method of tormenting her, Nash agreed smoothly, 'No, of course you haven't—from what I've heard from your besotted boss it seems that you managed to omit certain crucial facts from the CV you submitted to the Foundation.'

Faith knew exactly what he meant. Her throat dry with tension, she fought with all her emotional strength not to show him how afraid she now was.

'They had no relevance,' she insisted.

'No relevance? The fact that you only just escaped a custodial sentence; the fact that you were responsible for a man's death? Oh, no, you're staying right there,' Nash rasped as Faith, her self-control finally breaking, turned on her heel and tried to leave.

The shock of his fingers biting into the soft flesh of her upper arm caused her to cry out and demand frantically, 'Don't touch me.'

'Don't touch you?' Nash repeated. 'That's not what you used to say to me, is it, Faith? You used to plead with me to touch you…beg me…'

A low, tortured sound escaped Faith's trembling lips. 'I was fifteen—a child.' She tried to defend herself. 'I didn't know what I was saying—what I was doing…'

'Liar,' Nash contradicted her savagely, his free hand lifting to constrain her head and hold it so that she couldn't avoid meeting his eyes.

The sensation of Nash's lean fingers on her throat evoked a storm of reaction and remembrance. Her whole body started to shudder—not with fear, Faith recognised in shock, but with a heedless, wanton, inexplicable surge of feeling she had thought she had left behind her years ago.

How often that summer she had first seen Nash had she ached to have him touch her, *want* her? How many, many times had she fantasised then about him holding her captive like this? Imagining the brush of his fingers against her skin, picturing the feral glitter in his eyes as his gaze searched her face, his body hard with wanting her.

She shuddered again, acknowledging the naïvety of her long-ago teenage self. She had believed herself in love with Nash and had felt for him all the intense passion of that love, wanting to give herself to him totally and completely, longing for him, *aching* for him with all the ardour and innocence of youth.

'You don't know what you're talking about,' he had dismissed once, when she had been attempting to tell him how she felt and what she wanted.

'Then show me,' she had responded boldly, adding frantically, 'Kiss me, Nash.'

Nash froze in disbelief as he heard the words Faith had unwittingly whispered aloud, repeating her own thoughts. Kiss her? What kind of game was she trying to play? He started to move his hand away from her throat, but as he did so Faith turned her head, her lips grazing against his fingers.

Faith gasped as she felt the warm texture of Nash's flesh against her unguarded lips. She heard the low sound he made deep in his throat, felt him close the small gap that separated them, his body hard and undeniably male against the shocked softness of hers. His hand was pressed into the small of her back, imprisoning her against him, his mouth firm and cool as it covered hers—

Nash felt the shock of what he was doing all the way right down to his toes. Faith's body felt unbelievably vulnerable against his own, all soft womanly curves, her mouth sweet and warm. He could feel the temptation to touch her, give in to her, weakening him. His whole purpose in being here was to see justice done, to make sure she was punished for the crime she had committed. He owed it to his godfather to do that much at least for him—and yet here he was instead—

As he felt Faith's response to him Nash shuddered deeply, fighting to remind himself that the sweet, innocent girl he had so stupidly believed Faith was had never really existed, that the woman she was now knew *exactly* what she was doing and what effect she was having on him. But even telling himself that couldn't stop him from answering the passion in her kiss, the invitation of her softly parted lips.

When Faith felt the hot fierce thrust of Nash's tongue opening her lips, seeking the intimacy of her mouth, stroking sensually against her own tongue, she felt as though she was drowning in wave after wave of increasingly urgent desire. It filled her, stormed her, drew her down to a place of deep, dark, velvet sweetness, a place of hot, bold, dangerous, sensual savagery, a place where she and Nash…

She and Nash!

Faith suddenly realised what she was doing and immediately pulled herself free of Nash, her face flooding with the betraying colour of her distress and confusion, her eyes haunted and dark with the pain of it. She had kissed him as the girl she had been, loving the man *he* had been, Faith acknowledged as she tried to reconcile what she had just experienced in his arms with the reality of the enmity and distrust that now lay between them.

As she'd pulled away from him Nash had stepped back from her. Faith could see the way his chest was rising and falling with the harshness of his breathing, and she quailed beneath the bitter contemptuous look he was giving her.

'You're wasting your time trying those tactics on me, Faith,' she heard him saying cynically to her. 'They might work on other men, but I know what you're really like…'

'That's not true. I wasn't,' Faith defended herself passionately. 'You have no right—'

'Where you and I are concerned, Faith,' Nash cut across her warningly, 'right doesn't come into it.' What the hell was he doing? Angrily Nash reminded himself of just what Faith was.

Faith bit her bottom lip.

'My godfather had a right to have the trust he placed in you respected,' he continued grimly. 'And he also had a right to expect justice to be done—a right to have just payment made for his death.'

'I wasn't responsible for that,' Faith protested shakily. 'You can't make me—' You can't make me admit to something I didn't do, she had been about to say, but before she could do so Nash was interrupting her.

'I can't make you what, Faith?' he asked her with soft venom. 'I can't make you pay? Oh, I think you'll find that I can. You've already admitted that you lied by omission on your CV to the Ferndown

Foundation. Given their much-publicised belief in old-fashioned moral standards, you must know as well as I do that there's no way you would have got that job if they'd known the truth. Oh, I'm not trying to say that Ferndown himself wouldn't have still taken you to bed, but I think we both know it would have been a very different kind of business arrangement he'd have offered.'

'I was never convicted.' Faith tried to defend herself helplessly. She felt as though she had strayed into a horrific waking nightmare. Never had she imagined anything like this might happen. She had always known how much Nash blamed and hated her, of course, but to discover that he was now bent on punishing her as he believed the law had failed to do threw her into a state of mind-numbing panic.

'No, you weren't, were you?' Nash agreed, giving her an ugly look.

Faith swallowed against the torturous dryness of her aching throat. Someone had interceded on her behalf, pleaded for clemency for her and won the sympathy and compassion of the juvenile court so that all she had received was a suspended sentence. She'd never known who that person was, and no one would ever know just how heavy she found the burden of the guilt she had denied to Nash. No one— and most of all not the man now so cruelly confronting and threatening her.

'You *knew* I was coming here,' was all she could manage to say, her voice cracking painfully against the dryness of her throat.

'Yes. I knew,' Nash agreed coolly. 'That was a cunning move of yours, to claim that you had no close family or friends to supply a character reference for you and to give the name of your university tutor—a man who only knew that part of your life that came after my godfather's death.'

'I did that because there *wasn't* anyone else,' Faith responded sharply. 'It had nothing to do with being cunning. My mother was my only family, and she…she died.' She stopped, unable to go on. Her mother had lost her long battle against her heart condition two days after Faith had heard the news of Philip Hatton's death, which was why she had not been able to attend his funeral.

'Well, it certainly seems that your tutor thought highly of you,' Nash continued, giving her a thin-lipped, disparaging smile. 'Did you offer yourself to him just like you did to me, Faith?'

'No!' Her voice rang with repugnance, her feelings too strong for her to conceal and too overwhelming for her to notice the glitter that touched Nash's eyes before he turned away from her.

When Robert had been briefing her about the project he had told her that the house was being looked after by a skeleton staff whom the Foundation would keep on whilst it was being converted, and Faith tensed now, as the housekeeper walked into the study.

She wasn't the same housekeeper Faith remembered from all those years ago, and, giving Faith a cold stare, she turned away from her to Nash and told him, 'I've made up your usual room for you, Mr Nash, and I've put the young lady in the room you indicated. I've left a cold supper in the fridge, but if you want me to come in during the evening whilst you're here...'

'Thank you, Mrs Jenson.' Nash smiled. 'But that won't be necessary.'

Faith stared at the housekeeper's departing back, her heart sinking as she recognised the other woman's antagonism towards her. But she had more important concerns to address right now—far more important! Swinging round to confront Nash, she whispered, white-faced, 'You can't stay *here*.'

The smile he gave her sent another burst of white-hot fear licking along her veins.

'Oh, yes, I can,' he told her softly. 'I made it a condition of the hand-over, and naturally the Foundation's board fully understood that I would want to oversee the conversion. Especially since it was being handled by such an inexperienced young architect.'

Faith looked blindly at him. 'But I'm staying here—I have to—it's all arranged. You can't do this to me,' she protested. 'It's...it's harassment,' she accused him wildly. 'It's...'

'Justice,' Nash supplied with soft deadliness.

CHAPTER TWO

'I'VE instructed Mrs Jenson to put you in your old room.'

Her old room. Hugging her arms around herself for protection, Faith recalled the openly challenging way in which Nash had delivered that piece of information. It had been obvious to her that he was expecting some kind of hostile reaction, but she refused to allow him to manipulate either her actions or her emotions.

Her old room. Pensively she walked across to the small window and looked down at the elegant mini-patchwork of the gardens.

This room had once been part of the house's original nursery, tucked away in the *faux* turret that formed such a distinctive part of the house's architecture. It was an amusing piece of fantasy on the part of its designer, and at fifteen Faith had still been young enough to imagine herself as a fairy tale princess, enjoying the solitude of her private tower.

'I expect you're disappointed that the tower isn't surrounded by a lake,' Nash had teased her when she had tried to express her pleasure at being given such a special room, but to Faith the tower room Philip Hatton had chosen for her was perfect as it was, and she had struggled to find the words to tell him so.

That night, her first night in the room's comfortable and generously proportioned bed, she had closed her eyes and thought about her mother, whispering to her in her thoughts, telling her how lucky she felt, describing the room to her and knowing how much pleasure her mother would have had in sharing with her the wonder of everything she was experiencing. She had wished passionately that her mother could be there with her.

But of course she couldn't. And tears had filled her eyes, Faith remembered, and she had cried silently into her pillow, knowing with the maturity that the last painful and frightening six months had brought her that her mother would *never* see Hatton.

Restlessly Faith moved away from the window. The room had hardly changed; the bed in it looked exactly the same as the one she remembered, although the curtains at the window and the covers on the bed were different. Even the faded old-fashioned rose-coloured wallpaper was the same. Tenderly she reached out and touched one of the roses.

Her bedroom in the tiny Housing Association flat she and her mother had shared had had pretty wallpaper. They had papered it together just after they moved in. She had known how much her mother had hated leaving the small cottage they had lived in since Faith's birth, but the garden had become too much for her and the flat had been closer to the hospital, and to Faith's school, and much easier for her mother, being on the ground floor.

There was something almost frightening about the power one event could have to change a person's whole life, Faith acknowledged now as her thoughts focused on the past. It had only been by the merest chance that she had ever come to Hatton at all.

Shortly after the move to their flat, her mother's doctor had announced that she had to have a major operation and that after it she would be sent to recuperate at a special rest home, where she would have to stay for several months.

At first her mother had flatly refused to agree. Faith had only been just fifteen, and there had been no way she could be left to live on her own for the time the doctors had said her recuperation would take. The doctor's response had been to suggest that the Social Services be approached to find a place for Faith temporarily at a local children's home, where she could stay until her mother was well enough to look after her.

At first her mother had refused to even consider such an option, but Faith had seen for herself just how rapidly and painfully her mother's health was deteriorating, and despite her own dread and fear she had set about convincing her mother that she was perfectly happy to do as the doctors were suggesting.

'It will only be for a while,' Faith had tried to reassure her mother. 'And it will be mostly during the summer holidays. It will be fun having some other girls to talk to…'

And so it had been arranged. But right at the last minute, on the very day that Faith's mother had been due to be admitted to hospital, it had been decided that instead of going to the local children's home Faith would have to be sent to one almost fifty miles away.

Faith could still remember how apprehensive she had felt, but her fear for her mother had been greater. Even worse had been the discovery that she would not be allowed to visit her mother, either after her operation or whilst she was recuperating.

Although on her arrival at the home the staff there had been kind, Faith had felt overwhelmed by the anonymous busyness of the place, and the hostility of one particular group of girls who had already been living there.

She had been allowed to speak to her mother by telephone after her operation, but Faith had determinedly said nothing about the crude attempts of this group of girls to bully her and demand money from her. The last thing she'd wanted was for her mother to worry about *her* when Faith knew she needed all her strength to get better.

A week after she had first arrived at the home Faith had been thrilled to discover that they were being taken out for the day to visit a nearby Edwardian mansion and its gardens. Her father had been an architect, and it had been her secret dream to follow in his footsteps—although with her

mother's meagre income she had known it was unlikely that she would ever be able to go to university
and get the necessary qualifications.

It had taken a little of her pleasure away to discover that the girls who had taken such an open
dislike to her were also going on the trip—as well
as surprising her, since they had all been extremely
and crudely vocal about *their* favourite ways of
spending their time.

Faith had known that her mother would be horrified if she knew about them. Faith had heard them
boasting openly about their criminal activities. She
had even heard whispers from some of the other
girls about them going into the local town and stealing from the shops there.

'Why don't you tell someone?' Faith had asked
the girl who had told her. The other girl had shuddered.

'They'd kill me if they found out, and anyway,
like Charlene says, even if they do get caught they'll
only be sent to a juvenile court.'

'Only!' Faith hadn't been able to conceal her own
shock, but the other girl had shrugged dismissively.

'Charlene's brother's already in a remand home.
She says he says it's great…they can do what they
like. He got sent there for stealing a car. Charlene
hates it here because she says there's nothing worth
thieving—only bits of stuff from shops.'

Faith had been appalled, and even more determined to give the girls in question a wide berth.
They'd seemed to take a delight in taunting and tor-

menting her, but her mother's illness had given her a maturity that had helped her to ignore them and to treat them with a dignified silence.

The theft from her room, though, of the delicate silver brooch her mother had given to her—a tiny little fairy—which had originally been given to her by Faith's father—had been very hard to bear. Especially when Faith had been pretty sure of who was responsible for taking it. She had reported her loss to the home's harassed staff, though she had sensed it was a waste of time.

Hatton was virtually within walking distance of the home, although they had been taken there by coach, and Faith could still remember the wave of delight that had swept her as she'd seen the house for the first time.

Designed by Lutyens, it had a magical, storybook air that had entranced Faith even whilst her quick intelligence had registered the architectural features favoured by the famous designer.

Whilst the other girls had hurried in bored impatience through the house Faith had lingered appreciatively over every room, and it had been when she had sneaked back for a second look at the study that Philip Hatton had found her.

He had been elderly then—in his mid-seventies—thin and ascetic-looking, with kind, wise eyes and a gentle smile, and Faith had been drawn to him immediately.

She had spent the rest of the afternoon with him, listening to him talk about the house and its history, drinking in every word and in return telling him about her own circumstances.

Much to the bemusement of the carer in charge of them, Philip had insisted that Faith was to remain after the others had left, to have tea with him.

'But how will she get back to the home?' the poor woman had protested.

'I shall send her back in my car,' Philip had responded.

Faith smiled now, remembering the lordly air which had been so much a part of him.

Faith could remember every tiny detail of that shared supper.

After sending her upstairs to 'wash her hands', in the kind care of his elderly housekeeper, Faith had returned to the study to find that Philip Hatton was no longer on his own.

'Ah, Faith.' Philip had beamed at her. 'Come in and meet my godson, Nash. He's spending the summer here with me. Nash, come and say hello to Faith. She's a fellow Lutyens fan.'

And so it had begun. One look at Nash, tall, impossibly good-looking, with his muscular sexy body and his shock of thick dark hair, his amazing topaz eyes and his stunning aura of male sensuality, and Faith had fallen headfirst in love. How could she not have done so?

They had dined on fresh asparagus, poached salmon and strawberries and cream—Philip's favourite summer supper, as she had later discovered—and even today the taste of salmon, the smell of strawberries always took her straight back to that meal.

It had seemed to her then that the very air in the room was drenched in some special magical light, some wonderful mystical golden glow, that suddenly she was grown-up, an adult, with both Philip and Nash listening attentively to her participation in their shared conversation.

The misery she had experienced at the home had been forgotten; she had felt somehow like a caterpillar, emerging from its constricting chrysalis to experience the exhilaration and freedom of flight.

It was Nash who had driven her back to the home. Faith could still remember the way her heart had started to race with frantic excitement when he had stopped the car just outside the entrance. It had been dark by then, and in the shadowy privacy of the quiet lane, seated next to Nash in the car, Faith had held her breath. Was he going to touch her...kiss her? Did he feel like she did?

A mirthless smile stretched the soft fullness of her mouth now as she relived her naïve emotions and the sharpness of her disappointment when Nash had simply thanked her for her kindness to his godfather.

'But I enjoyed talking to him,' she had insisted truthfully.

Less than a week after that she had been living full time at Hatton—an arrangement that had been made after Philip had written to her mother, inviting Faith to spend the rest of the school holidays at Hatton as his guest.

She had been speechless…ecstatic, unable to believe her good fortune when the news had been broken to her. If only she had known *then* what the outcome of her stay was to be…

Automatically Faith walked back to the window, pushing her memories away. From up here she had a wonderfully panoramic view of the Gertrude Jekyll-designed gardens that were at their very best at this time of the year. She could well remember the long sunny hours she had spent alongside Philip, weeding out the magnificent long borders either side of the path that led to the pretty summerhouse.

Faith froze as a large car pulled up outside the house and Nash got out. Where had he been? Had she known he was out she would have gone downstairs and got herself something to eat. She didn't want to eat with Nash.

Prior to her arrival Robert had told her that arrangements had been made for her to live in the house, but that she would have to fend for herself so far as meals were concerned.

'The kitchen is fully equipped, and you'll be able to make use of its facilities, but we shall also give you an allowance in order that you can eat out if you wish—and I hope you will wish.' Robert had smiled at her. 'Especially on those occasions when *I* come down to the house for our progress meetings.'

Faith had smiled, but Robert's interest in her was a complication she hadn't allowed for when she had initially applied for her job.

Faith believed she had every right not to inform her prospective employers about the events leading up to Philip's death. But to conceal them from someone with whom she might form a close personal relationship was something she would never consider doing.

To Faith, loving someone meant being honest with them, trusting them, and had she and Robert met in different circumstances she knew there would have come a stage in their relationship when she would have wanted to open up to him about her past.

She liked Robert. Of course she did. And, yes, one day she hoped to marry and have children. But... A troubled frown furrowed her forehead.

Why had Nash had to reappear in her life? She shivered as she remembered the way he had looked at her when he had told her that he was determined to seek justice for Philip's death.

Inadvertently her gaze was drawn downward, to where Nash was striding towards the house, and as though some mysterious force linked them together he stopped and lifted his head, his gaze unerringly focusing on the tower and her window.

Immediately Faith stepped back, but she knew that Nash had seen her.

The summer she had stayed here she had spent more time than she wanted to remember waiting...watching for Nash to arrive. From here there was an excellent view of the drive, and in those days Nash had driven a racy little scarlet sports car.

Although officially he had been spending the

summer helping his godfather, he had also, even then, been working on the business venture upon which he had eventually built his current empire.

In those days whenever he'd seen her watching for him he would stand underneath her window and smile up at her, teasingly telling her that if she wasn't careful one day he might scale the wall to reach her.

Faith had prayed that he might, so deeply in love with him by then that there had scarcely been any room in her thoughts or her emotions for anyone else but him. He had been her ideal, her hero, and as the girl in her had given way to the growing woman her longing for him had increased and intensified.

From hardly daring to look at his mouth, for fear of blushing because of her desire to feel its hard male strength against her own, she had found herself focusing boldly on it, the words she had known she must never speak pleading in silent longing inside her head.

Kiss me.

Well, today, ten years too late, he *had* kissed her, but not as she had longed for him, *dreamed* of him doing then, with love and tenderness, a look of bemused adoration in his eyes as he begged her for her love. Oh, no. The kiss he had given her today had been hard, angry, pulsing with the violence of his emotions and his antagonism towards her.

So why, then, had she responded to it with a passion that she had never given to any of the other men she had dated?

The sharp irritation of her inner voice unnerved her. She had responded to him because her memories had tricked her, that was all. She had thought…forgotten… She had *believed* that it was Nash as she had once imagined him to be that she was kissing. And as for those other men—well, they had just been casual dates, nothing serious, and she had kissed them more out of a sense of fair play than anything else. Kisses were all that she had *wanted* to share with them.

Only with Robert had she sensed that maybe… just maybe something deeper and stronger might eventually grow to life between them. But these days Faith was very protective of her emotions, very cautious about who she allowed into her life. These days a man like Nash Connaught would have no chance whatsoever of bedazzling her into making the same dangerous mistakes she had made at fifteen.

So far as Faith was concerned now, the most important cornerstone for a relationship was mutual trust. Without that… Without that there could be nothing—or nothing that *she* would want, that she would ever consider worth having, as she had good and bitter cause to know.

In her bleakest moments after the death of Philip and her mother the only thing that had kept her going had been the knowledge that Philip *had* trusted her—enough to make that wonderfully unexpected provision in his will for her.

When she had first learned that Philip had left money specially to finance her studies and her passage through university Faith had hardly been able to believe it. Prior to that she had told herself that the only way she had any hope whatsoever of qualifying as an architect would be to find herself a job and then study in her spare time, which she had known meant that her goal would be virtually impossible for her to reach.

But it hadn't just been the discovery that Philip had left her the money that had meant so much to her. What had mattered even more was knowing that despite everything that had happened he had, after all, believed in her. There was, in Faith's opinion, no price that could be put on that. It was a gift *beyond* price; a gift so precious that even now just to think about it filled her eyes with tears and an emotion she knew someone like Nash would *never* in a million lifetimes be able to understand.

Nash, to whom everything was black or white… Nash, who could condemn a person without allowing them to defend themselves… Nash, in whose eyes she was a thief and a murderer…

Angrily Nash headed towards the house. Just for a heartbeat then, seeing Faith standing at the window, the sunlight dancing on her hair, lingering on its stunning and unique mixture of differing shades of blonde, from purest silver to warmest gold, he had been inexorably swept back in time.

He had known right from the moment his godfather had announced that he intended to invite her to spend the summer at Hatton that she spelled trouble, but he hadn't imagined then just how fatally accurate his prediction was going to be. The kind of trouble he had anticipated had had *nothing* to do with theft and...and murder.

His mouth hardened, the expression in his eyes bleak. Like his godfather, he had been totally taken in by Faith, believing her to be a naïve young girl, never imagining... Bitterness joined the bleakness in his eyes. Hell, he had even wanted to *protect* her, believing then that her advances to him were totally innocent and that she'd had no idea of what she was really inviting when she'd looked at him, her face burning hot with the thoughts he could see so plainly in those limpid dark blue eyes.

He had even derived a certain amount of painful amusement from the way she'd looked at his mouth, semi-boldly, semi-shyly, but wholly provocatively, wondering just what she would do if he actually responded to her invitation and gave in to the fierce heat of desire she was creating inside him.

But she had been fifteen, a child, as he had sternly and furiously reminded himself more times than he cared to count during that brief summer, and no matter how much his body might have reacted, telling him in increasingly urgent and physical terms just how *it* viewed her, his mind had known that to give in to what he was feeling would have been dishonourable and wrong.

She would not always be fifteen, he had told himself. One day she *would* be adult, and then... Then he would make her pay over and over again for every one of those naïvely tormenting looks she had given him, pay in kiss after kiss for all those kisses he had ached to steal from her but had known he must not.

How many nights had he lain awake, tormented by the heat of his own need, virtually unable to stop himself from groaning out aloud at the thought of how she would feel lying against him? Her skin silken soft, her mouth as perfect and perfumed as Gertrude Jekyll's warmly scented roses, her eyes as blue as the campanula that grew amongst them. God, but he had wanted her, ached for her, longed for her. Hell, he had even been stupid enough to make plans for his future that had included her...for *their* future...

Initially not even to himself had he dared to acknowledge just how much he'd looked forward to seeing her waiting for him, standing at her turret window, a modern-day Rapunzel imprisoned away from him, not by her father but by her age and his own moral convictions.

It had left a residue of bitterness to be forced to recognise that the innocence he had striven so hard to protect from his own desire had been little more than a fiction created to conceal the real Faith. But his personal bitterness was nothing to the anguish and the anger he felt on behalf of his godfather. The anguish, the anger and the guilt. If he had not been so bemused by Faith, nor so wrapped up in the excitement of beginning the property empire that had now made him such a wealthy man, he might have seen more clearly what was happening and what Faith really was.

But there was no way he was going to fall into that same trap a second time.

The shock of discovering that she was working for the very foundation he had chosen to benefit from his godfather's bequest had caused him to take the first flight from New York to London, despite the fact that he had been in the middle of lengthy discussions involving the sale of leases on some of his most expensive properties. His initial intention had been to warn Robert Ferndown of just what Faith was, but then he had heard Robert eulogising about her abilities, and Faith herself, and he had been caught up in a flood of savage anger against her.

It had been then that he had decided to punish her for the crime she had committed, to punish her not swiftly and immediately, with a clean, sharp cut, but to give her a taste of what his godfather had suffered...to keep her on a knife-edge of fear and dread, never knowing when the final blow was going to fall.

He let himself into the house and paused as he walked past the open study door. He could still taste

Faith's kiss on his lips, still almost feel her against
his body, feel his own unwanted reaction to her.
Angrily he turned on his heel. What the hell was he
trying to do to himself?

CHAPTER THREE

FAITH flexed her fingers and moved tiredly away from her laptop. It was still far too early for her to begin her preliminary report on the house, but looking down into the garden had reminded her not just of the pretty little summer house but of the many statues in the garden as well, some of which she knew were extremely valuable.

She would have to check with Robert to see whether or not they were to remain in the garden, and if they were how best they could be protected from damage and theft. Tomorrow she would list them all properly and contact Robert to get his advice.

She tensed as she heard a knock on her door, knowing who it would be and hesitating warily before going to answer it.

'Yes?' she questioned Nash hardly as she saw him standing outside the door.

He had changed his clothes since she had seen him getting out of his car and was now wearing a white tee shirt that clung to his torso in a way that suddenly made her feel far too hot. She could almost feel her face burning as her senses reacted to the maleness of him. As a girl she had adored him, longed for him, *worshipped* him almost, but now, as a woman, she was aware of the air of raw sexuality that clung to him—aware of it and resentful of it too.

'The supper Mrs Jenson left is still in the fridge. She'll be offended if we don't eat it,' Nash told her abruptly.

The words 'I'm not hungry' were burning on the tip of Faith's tongue, but before she could say them her traitorous tummy gave a very audible and very hungry gurgle.

Unable to meet Nash's eyes, Faith told him tersely, 'I'll be down shortly. I'm just finishing something.'

Faith waited until she was sure he had gone before racing to close her bedroom door. Her hands were trembling violently. Was she imagining it or could she really scent danger in the air? Danger and something else—something that was wholly and hormone-activatingly Nash.

She quickly sluiced her hot face in the bathroom that adjoined her bedroom, brushed her hair and reapplied the minimal amount of make-up she favoured. After what he had said to her she could scarcely believe that Nash had actually bothered to concern himself about the fact that she had not had any supper. Or perhaps he wanted to make sure she ate it where he could ensure that she didn't make off with the cutlery and crockery, she told herself cynically.

And yet when she walked into the kitchen and discovered that it was empty of Nash's presence her predominant feeling was one of…of what? she asked herself sharply. Not disappointment…no way. No, she was *glad* he was at least giving her the privacy to eat alone, without his tormenting presence.

But as she opened the fridge she realised she was wrong, because Nash was walking into the kitchen.

'Asparagus and salmon,' Faith murmured as she saw the food that had been left for them. Her eyes filmed with tears, forcing her to keep her head down so that Nash couldn't see them whilst she blinked fiercely to disperse them.

Philip's favourites.

Suddenly Faith knew that despite her hunger the food would taste like sawdust to her.

Shakily she closed the fridge door.

'I've changed my mind,' she told Nash. 'I'm not hungry.'

The look of male incomprehension he gave her might have amused her under different circumstances, but when she headed for the kitchen door she saw it change to frowning anger as Nash moved lithely past her to stand between her and her exit.

'I don't know what kind of game you think you're playing—' he began ominously.

Faith felt her self-control starting to fray. It had been a long day, beginning with her being buoyed up with excitement and pride at the knowledge that Robert had entrusted her with such an important project, then going from that to deep, numbing shock when she had first seen Nash. Then had come the trauma of reliving searingly painful memories—and that was without taking into account everything she had experienced when Nash had kissed her.

'*I'm* not the one who's playing games,' she refuted fiercely, her voice trembling with the intensity of her feelings. 'You're the one who's doing *that*, Nash. Why have you come here? Why are you *staying* here? That wasn't part of the arrangement Robert made with the trustees of the estate.'

'You seem to know an awful lot about his business for a relatively new employee,' Nash countered smoothly, and Faith suspected that despite her anger he could tell that underneath it she was feeling very vulnerable. 'But then, of course, you *aren't* just his employee, are you, Faith? Why the hell do you *think* I'm here?' he demanded with an abrupt change of tone. 'Do you really think for one moment that once I learned *you'd* be here I would allow you to stay on your own?

'This house is full of almost priceless architectural features—panelling, architraves, fireplaces, to name just a few items that would fetch thousands if they were removed and sold to some unscrupulous builder who wasn't worried about checking where they'd come from.'

Faith knew that what he was saying was true, but it appalled her that he should actually consider her capable of perpetrating such a crime. Before she could defend herself Nash was attacking her again, although in a very different way this time.

'Are you going to tell *Robert* that you asked me to kiss you?' he asked with acid softness.

'What? I...I did no such thing,' Faith denied with vehement indignation, her face pink with anger.

'Liar,' Nash taunted her. '"Kiss me"—that's what you said to me.' His mouth twisted. 'Although of course it's typical of you that you should deny it.'

Her face was now scarlet with mortification as she had a sickening memory of actually *thinking* those words. Surely she hadn't...*couldn't* have said them out aloud? But she must have done—unless Nash had read her mind, which in truth she wouldn't entirely put past him.

'The next thing you'll be doing is trying to pretend that you didn't enjoy it,' Nash goaded her tauntingly.

Now Faith really *had* had enough.

'I didn't,' she denied flatly.

'No? Well, there's one very sure way to prove whether or not you're telling the truth, isn't there?' Nash retaliated.

The way he was watching her, looking at her like a hungry lion eyeing up its prey, made Faith wish with all her heart that she had never become involved in a verbal battle she knew Nash would not allow her to win.

'Fortunately for me Hatton doesn't have a torture chamber,' she told him with angry scorn.

'I don't *need* a torture chamber to prove you a

liar,' Nash told her smoothly. '*This* is all it's going to take…'

Faith's eyes widened in disbelief as he took hold of her, imprisoning her against his body and holding her captive there as he bent his head.

Grittily she closed her lips tightly together, fiercely refusing to close her eyes, letting them tell him all that her lips could not as they glittered with angry contempt and female pride, daring him to do his worst.

'Open your mouth.' Nash seemed impervious to the intensity of the rage and hostility emanating from her tense body. 'Open your mouth Faith,' he repeated as he drew his tongue-tip oh, so lightly across the closed line of her lips.

The sensual way in which the warm, wet tip of his tongue was stroking almost lovingly against her lips was so shockingly distracting that Faith found her thoughts releasing their hold on her anger and sliding with shaming wantonness to concentrate instead on the sensations Nash's expertly seductive attack was having on her.

If she closed her eyes that sensation magnified a hundredfold, and that surely *must* be the reason she was starting to tremble as treacherously as a young girl experiencing her first real awareness of what a kiss could be. But Nash wasn't even kissing her yet—not really. He was just playing with her, teasing her, *tormenting* her. She could feel his breath against her skin, smell the unique Nash smell of him, feel…

On a low moan of defeat Faith didn't even know she was making, her lips started to part.

Achingly Faith clung to Nash, her mouth moving eagerly against his, her hand sliding behind his head so that she could hold him close to her.

Nash, Nash... Silently she breathed his name in a sharp female cry that held all the pent-up longing of her teenage desire, of the nights when she had lain awake aching for him without knowing exactly what it was she was aching for. She had known about the mechanics of sex, of course, but the actuality of it had still been a mystery to her, and she had passionately believed Nash was the only man who could ever hold the key to unlock that mystery for her.

Had been a mystery?

Faith shuddered and felt the sharp intake of breath Nash made, as though somehow that fierce reaction of her body had affected his.

They were kissing as she had so often imagined they might, their mouths clinging, stroking, tasting, caressing, feasting, and the little murmurs of appreciative pleasure she could hear herself making were running through their kisses in a soft, disjointed paean of pleasure.

Then, abruptly, shockingly, Nash was pushing her away from him, his chest rising and falling sharply as he demanded in a voice that grated against her ears, 'How much more do I have to do to prove you a liar, Faith? Take you to bed? You'd certainly have let me.'

Appalled, sickened, disbelieving, Faith could only stand blank-eyed and shamed as he denounced her. She could offer him no defence nor any explanation. White-faced, her eyes huge and dark with pain and humiliation, she didn't know which of them she hated the most. Him or herself.

Nauseously she waited for the blow to fall, for Nash to tell her that he fully intended to reveal to Robert what she had done, but sinisterly he made no move to do so.

Faith could feel her anxiety start to increase. Her stomach was churning, her head ached and her eyes felt gritty and sore from the tears she refused to allow herself to cry.

'Where do you think you're going?' Nash demanded as she turned on her heel and hurried blindly towards the kitchen door.

'My room. I'm tired and I want to go to bed,' Faith told him shakily. 'Not that it's any business of yours, Nash. I'm not answerable to you. You don't have any control over me.'

There was the smallest pause before he responded, his voice silken with a menace that made the tiny hairs lift on the back of Faith's neck.

'No? Oh, I think you'll find that you are very *much* answerable to me, Faith, and that I have a *great* deal of control over you. If, for instance, I were to tell Robert what you had just done…'

'If?' Faith couldn't manage to keep the note of soft pleading out of her voice as she turned round to confront him.

'I thought you wanted to go to bed,' Nash taunted her smoothly.

He was enjoying this, Faith recognised. Well, she wasn't going to give him the satisfaction of pleading with him...begging him...

'I do,' she agreed fiercely, turning her back on him, walking determinedly towards the door and opening it.

As he watched her departing back Nash finally let out the pent-up breath he had been holding.

Where the *hell* had she learned to kiss like *that*...and who with...?

No other woman had *ever* kissed him like that, as if he was their life, their soul, their one desire. Their soul mate for this life and every life to come, their world...their everything. She had kissed him as though she had waited out an eternity for him...as though she had been starving for him...as though she loved him and only him.

A woman like Faith was a living, breathing mortal danger to a man when she kissed him like that. A woman like Faith...

Angrily Nash tried to dismiss her from his thoughts. Hadn't what she had done to his godfather taught him *anything*? Of course it had! What was she trying to do? Offer him sex to prevent him from telling Ferndown about her?

Alongside his anger and contempt Nash could feel the sharp savage heat that burned through his body. How could he *possibly* want her, given all that he knew about her? He had never merely wanted a

woman for sex. *Never.* And he *didn't* want Faith—
not really. It was just his mind playing tricks on him.
Some bizarre and treacherous effect of seeing her
here at Hatton and reactivating memories of the past.
A past when he *had* wanted her.

How many men had there been in her life since
then? How many men had experienced the dangerous witchery of her? If that kiss she had given him
was anything to go by…no wonder Ferndown was
so besotted with her!

But he had come here to finally put the past to
rest, Nash reminded himself savagely—not to reac-
tivate it.

Upstairs in her room Faith sank down onto her bed,
wrapping her arms protectively around her body as
she rocked herself helplessly to and fro.

Why, why, why had she allowed it to happen?
Why had she betrayed everything that she held most
dear? Why had she allowed herself to forget reality,
and, most important of all, why had she become so
bemused, so intoxicated, so entranced and so lost in
Nash's kiss? She had given in to his hands a powerful weapon for him to use against her, and given
it to him as carelessly and recklessly as she had once
given him her heart and her love.

She should never have come back here—would
never have come back here if she had guessed for
one moment that Nash was going to be here.

Ten years ago he had told her that he would never
forgive her for his godfather's death, but she had

never dreamed that he would pursue her for vengeance in the way he was now doing.

Downstairs in the kitchen Nash looked at the remains of his virtually uneaten meal. Grimly he got up and took the plate over to the pedal bin, removing the food before rinsing the plate and stacking it in the dishwasher.

Salmon had always been one of his godfather's favourite foods. Towards the end of his life it had become increasingly difficult for him to feed himself—a legacy of his stroke—and Nash could remember visiting him on his birthday and finding him close to tears of anger and pride as he had stared at the salmon on his plate.

In the end Nash had fed him himself, dismissing his nurse. It had been the least he could do. Philip had been like the grandfather Nash had never had, his home a refuge to Nash during his schooldays when his own parents had been out of the country. His father had been a foreign correspondent with a national newspaper and his mother a photographer. They, like Philip, were dead now, killed in an uprising in one of the countries they had been reporting from.

Philip had adored Faith, once confiding in Nash that she was the granddaughter he would have loved to have had. He had shown that love for her in his will, which he had altered with Nash's own knowledge and approval only days before he had been attacked. He had made a provision in it for a sum

to be set aside from his estate to pay for Faith's
further education; Nash knew that had he lived it
would have been Philip's intention to finance Faith
through a degree.

All three of them had shared a compelling interest
in architecture; in fact it had been Nash's own love
of interesting buildings which had led to him ac-
quiring his first property whilst he was still at
Oxford. He had bought a small row of terraced
houses with the money he had inherited from his
parents' estate, back then more because he had been
amused by their innovative and attractive early
Edwardian design than because he had wanted to
make money from them by letting them—that had
come later.

At least Faith had not lied to Philip about her
desire to become an architect. Nash frowned as he
remembered how determinedly his godfather had
battled with the after-effects of his stroke to make
sure Nash knew he wanted his will to stand. People
had assumed, because Philip lived in a large house,
that he was a wealthy man.

Nash's frown deepened. It was nearly midnight.
Time he was in bed.

It had taken Faith a long time to finally get off to
sleep, her body tense, her mind racing. And now a
dog fox, padding across the gardens, paused and
lifted his head, baying to the moon. In her sleep
Faith trembled, tormented by the darkness of her
dreams, their grip on her so intense that when the

fox's cry first woke her she actually thought that she was still fifteen, and was relieved to find herself here in her bed at Hatton, not in her room at the home.

The home!

As she sat up in the bed Faith clasped her hands round her knees and stared morosely towards the window. She had hated the home so much. Or rather she had hated the things she had experienced whilst she was living there.

Her mother's recovery had been progressing much more slowly than anyone had envisaged, and in September, when the new school year had begun, Faith had had to move back into the home from Hatton and attend school with the other girls.

The school her age group had attended had been in the local town—they'd travelled there and back every day by bus—and, as Faith had quickly discovered, girls from the home were considered troublemakers by the staff at school.

When her teachers had discovered that Faith genuinely wanted to work and learn she had earned their approbation and admiration—and the increased enmity of the home's dominating gang of girl bullies.

No one had been more astonished than Faith when, after weeks of tormenting and deriding her, one of the gang had approached her and invited her to join them on a Saturday morning shopping trip into town. Naïvely eager to accept the olive branch she was being offered, Faith had accepted. She'd had no money of her own to spend, but had been happy to take one of the other girl's goods and money to the checkout to pay for them.

It had only been once they were back outside in the street that Faith had discovered their real purpose in befriending her. They had started to shriek with laughter and jeer at her, boasting that they had used her as a decoy whilst they had been shoplifting.

Faith had been horrified, pleading with them to take the stolen goods back—make-up, in the main— which had only made them worse.

'*Pay* for it? Why should we when we can get it for free?' she had been told.

And as Faith had looked unhappily at them she had suddenly been uncomfortably aware of the narrow-eyed attention she was getting from the girl who was the leader of the small group.

Slightly older than the others, with—if the home's gossip was to be believed—a family background of theft, she had marched over to Faith, taking a handful of her hair and tugging it viciously as she'd warned her, 'Don't even think of snitching on us, Miss Posh, 'cos if you do…'

She had stopped whilst Faith had gritted her teeth against the pain. Her eyes had been beginning to water, but she'd been determined not to let the other girl see how much she was hurting her.

''Cos if you do,' the older girl had continued, giving Faith's hair an even more vicious tug, 'we'll just tell them that it was all your idea in the first place. Bet that old geezer up at the big house is filthy rich, isn't he? Bet that place is *loaded* down with stuff. How many tellys has he got?'

Faith had shaken her head and responded honestly, 'I don't know.'

Philip hadn't watched a lot of television, preferring to read.

'Keep much money up there, does he?' her tormentor had demanded. 'I bet he does. And don't tell me you haven't looked or been tempted to take a few quid, Miss Goody-two-shoes,' she had sneered.

'No,' Faith had protested, grateful that the arrival of their bus meant that the other girl had been forced to let her go.

'Just remember,' she had hissed as they got on the bus, 'try telling on us and you'll be for it, good and proper...'

Completely wide awake now, and fully back in the present, Faith hugged her knees.

Her conscience had troubled her very badly over the fact that she had not told anyone in authority about the shoplifting. It hadn't been fear that had stopped her—or at least not any fear of being physically hurt. It had been more her fear of betraying the youthful code of not 'telling tales' that had kept her silent. There *had* been a moment when she had been tempted to confide in one person, though, she acknowledged.

Closing her eyes, she expelled her breath shakily.

The following weekend she had been invited over to Hatton, and Nash had picked her up.

'What's wrong, Shrimp?' he had asked her, in that

teasing manner he'd sometimes adopted towards her which had made her itch to tell him that she was almost grown up, certainly grown up enough to know that she loved him.

'It's…' she had begun hesitantly, but just as she had struggled to find the words to tell him what had happened she'd realised that his attention had been distracted away from her by a stunningly beautiful brunette walking on the other side of the road.

Bringing his car to a halt, Nash had wound down the window and called out a greeting to the other woman.

The smile she had given him had confirmed Faith's view that Nash was just the most gorgeously hunky, sexy man there was, and when the brunette had crossed the road to indulge in some sophisticated banter with Nash, Faith had subsided into her seat, feeling forlorn and unwanted.

It had only been as Nash had finally driven away that she'd realised, despite the girl's open hints, Nash had *not* made any definite plans to take her out, and in the soaring surge of relief and joy that knowledge had brought, the dilemma she had been about to seek his advice on had been pushed to one side.

There had been many occasions in the decade since then when Faith had wondered just how different her life might have been if she had told him.

Just for a second silent tears glistened betrayingly in her eyes, but very quickly and determinedly she blinked them away. She had stopped crying over Nash Connaught a long, long time ago—hadn't she?

CHAPTER FOUR

'END of laburnum tunnel, nymph with water pot'.

As she wrote down her description of the statue she was standing in front of Faith sighed a little ruefully. This morning, when she had initially embarked on her self-imposed task, she hadn't realised just how many pieces of statuary and ornament the garden possessed, nor how much being in it was going to affect her and awaken more memories she had thought long ago safely buried.

But was it being in the garden that had awakened them or was it Nash? Nash and that insane, inexplicable response she had allowed him to steal from her last night?

Stop thinking about it, Faith warned herself fiercely. Stop thinking about *him*!

It was, after all, *Philip* who had first introduced her to the beauty of Hatton's gardens, and Nash had come walking towards them down the laburnum tunnel, the brief darts of sunlight that had pierced its summer-green canopy splashing splodges of lighter colour on the tee shirt he had been wearing—a tee shirt which she remembered far too vividly had openly revealed the smooth tanned column of his throat and the muscular strength of his forearms.

Just watching him then had made her go faint

with love and longing. That had been the occasion, she remembered—how could she possibly ever forget?—when Philip had suggested that Nash should take her to Oxford for dinner.

Faith had been speechless with embarrassment and excitement, scarcely daring to breathe as she had prayed that Nash would agreed.

'Do you like Italian food?' he had asked her.

Faith suspected she would have agreed to like any kind of food so long as she could eat it in his company, and now, recalling the incident, she could vividly see in her memory an image of Nash's face, and the quizzical amusement she had not really recognised then when she had breathed her fervent assent.

Oh, yes, Nash had known exactly how she had felt about him. But then she hadn't made any attempt to hide her feelings...her love...had she?

Nash had driven her to Oxford in his bright red sports car, and if he had felt resentful about the way his godfather had manipulated him into taking her out, there had been nothing in his manner towards her to betray it.

They had been having a good summer weather-wise. The evening had been soft and balmy, Oxford's streets busy with visitors while the colleges were empty of students for the long summer holiday. Nash had parked the car close to his own college, and Faith had studied both it and the other wonderful buildings they had walked past on their way to the restaurant with awed eyes. So much of the country's history had its roots in the early lives of those who had studied here: artists, writers, statesmen and women.

The Italian restaurant had been situated in a pretty courtyard off a narrow lane, and the *patrone*, a jocular middle-aged Italian, had shown them to a table which had afforded them a prime view of the other diners whilst giving them their own privacy.

It had been the first time she had eaten proper Italian food, the first time she had even been to a restaurant really, and Nash had laughed teasingly at her as she had struggled with her ribbons of pasta before moving closer to her and demonstrating the correct way to eat it.

Watching him twirl the pasta onto his fork had been one thing—trying to imitate him had been something else, and in the end...

Helplessly Faith closed her eyes. All too quickly and easily she was fifteen again, seated next to Nash in the restaurant. She could smell the fresh clean scent of his hair...his body... She knew it was Nash's scent because she had sneaked into his bathroom one afternoon when he hadn't been there just so that she could breathe in the special smell she always associated with him. She had even dampened a piece of cotton wool and put some of his shower gel onto it, secreting it beneath her own pillow so that when she went to bed the last thing she smelt at night and the first thing she smelt in the morning was Nash.

'No, not like that.' He had smiled when he'd seen

the way she was fumbling to copy him, adding, 'Here, let me show you.'

And then, unbelievably, his hand had been over hers as she'd held the fork and he'd moved her hand.

'Think you've got it now?' he'd asked her several dizzyingly blissful seconds later. 'Or do I have to feed you?' he had teased.

At fifteen she had been far too young and innocent to respond sexually to such a question—and anyway she had known that Nash had not intended it to be a sensual invitation for him to feed her as a *lover*—but she had not been too young to experience a sudden clutching, piercing sensation deep down inside her body, and neither had she been old enough to stop herself from gazing adoringly into Nash's eyes, her heart and feelings in her own.

No doubt *that* had been the reason he had very firmly removed his hand from hers and moved his chair back to its original position, saying crisply, 'Perhaps you should have ordered something it would be easier for you to eat.'

But not even that remark had had the power to quench her euphoric joy, Faith remembered.

The subtle adult nuances of Nash's manner towards her, which had been lost on her at fifteen, deep in the throes of the passionate intensity of a love she was longing to have returned, were revealed to her in sharp painful clarity now as she reran her mental recording of that time past her now adult awareness.

What she had seen as a uniquely romantic evening shared by two people who were destined to love one another had no doubt to Nash simply been the execution of a duty.

It had been growing dark later, when they had walked back to the car side by side, with Faith as close to Nash's side as she had dared. Nash himself had somehow or other managed to keep a few inches of space between their bodies, but then they had had to cross a very busy intersection, where the traffic lights, for some reason, hadn't been working, and Nash had reached out and taken her hand.

To share such a physical intimacy with him twice in one evening had put Faith on such a high plateau of intense emotion that she hadn't been able to imagine she could possibly feel any happier—unless, of course, Nash had fulfilled her wildest dreams and actually kissed her.

Her wildest dreams?

The reality of Nash's kiss had been more like her worst nightmare, Faith thought bitterly now as she headed for the elegant Italian garden, with its box hedges and formal fishpond.

Philip had told her that the ornaments in this garden had actually originally come from Italy. Boys astride dolphins, with water spouting from the dolphins' mouths, decorated each corner of the pond, which was large enough not to be overwhelmed by the intricate fountain at its centre.

Steps would have to be taken to protect visiting children from the dangers of the pond, Faith acknowledged as she wrote a quick note on her pad before beginning to list the garden's ornaments.

As she did so she noticed that one of the dolphins looked slightly different from the others. Frowning, she went over to make a closer examination of it. Both its colour and composition were different, she recognised as she knelt down to inspect it even more closely.

'If you're planning what I *think* you're planning, you can forget it. Someone's already tried it and that's the result. The dolphin *he* was trying to steal ended up smashed and the one *you're* inspecting is its replacement.'

The unexpected sound of Nash's harsh voice caught Faith off guard. Immediately she stood up and turned to confront him as the meaning of his tautly angry words hit her.

But without giving her a chance to say anything Nash continued coldly, 'What exactly *are* you doing out here anyway, Faith? I thought your task was supposed to be preparing a plan for the house conversion, not checking out the garden—and its contents!'

'I wanted to make a list of all the garden ornaments,' Faith cut across his sarcastic comment in quick defence.

But before she could finish her explanation Nash had stopped her again, exclaiming derisively, 'Oh, I'm sure you did. But unfortunately for you I happened to see what you were up to. As I've already told you, someone else had the same idea before you and tried to make off with these four.' He gestured towards the dolphins.

'I wasn't—' Faith began angrily, but once again Nash refused to allow her to finish what she was saying.

'Your boss has been on the phone for you,' he told her. 'No doubt, like me, he expected to find you doing your job. He asked me to tell you that he'll be here later on today, and no doubt when he does arrive,' he continued smoothly, 'he's going to want a full report on how you've spent your time in his absence.'

She might have registered the sneering double meaning in Nash's speech, but there was no way she was going to give him the satisfaction of letting him know it, Faith decided firmly. And there was *one* point she fully intended to put him right on.

'For your information—' she began determinedly.

But to her fury yet again Nash took the initiative away from her, pre-empting her by saying harshly, 'For my information *what*? I already *have* all the information I need or want about anything *you* might do or say, Faith. Oh, and by the way, Mrs Jenson isn't here to cook and clean for you.'

That was it! Faith had had enough!

'What *is* she here for, Nash? To spy on me? Is that why I caught her in my room this morning?'

Faith could see from Nash's expression that he didn't like what she was saying. Tough! Did he *really* think he could get away with piling insult after insult on her without her retaliating?

'She was probably returning the laundry you'd left downstairs for her to wash,' Nash countered, frowning.

'You mean the laundry I'd left downstairs to put in the washing machine after it had finished the cycle it was on?' Faith corrected him, adding before he could cut her off, 'Wasn't the arrangement my company had with the trustees that whilst I was here I could use the domestic facilities of the house?'

'That doesn't include the services of a housekeeper,' Nash shot back at her.

'I was referring to the washing machine, not Mrs Jenson,' Faith told him sharply, pushing her hand into her hair in helpless irritation as she acknowledged the impossibility of having anything approximating a normal rational conversation with Nash.

But his comments had reminded her of something. 'It would be helpful if I could have a copy of any existing floor plan of the house you might have,' she told him stiffly.

'You mean it will save you the bother of drawing one up yourself—thus allowing you to spend your time far more profitably, from your point of view at least, in checking out the property's more moveable and readily disposable assets. Well, for your information—'

'No. For *your* information,' Faith interrupted him swiftly, copying his own aggressive method of attack, 'let me tell you that the only reason I was looking at the garden ornaments is because...'

As she was speaking a sudden breeze caught at

the pages of the notebook she had put down beside
her on the ground, drawing Nash's attention to it.

Instinctively Faith bent to pick it up, but Nash
moved even faster, and the expression in his eyes as
he studied the list she had made was so contemp-
tuously damning that for some idiotic reason it made
Faith want to cry.

'Don't say another word,' Nash advised her as he
calmly tore the list she had made in half, and then
in half again. 'I'm just glad that Philip didn't live
to see what you've become. He *trusted* you, Faith.'

'And I have *never* abused his trust—' Faith began
passionately, and then stopped as she saw the way
Nash was watching her. What was the point in even
trying to talk to him? Instead she simply turned on
her heel and walked as quickly as she could back to
the house.

Faith was feeling rather pleased with herself. A trip
into the local town after her run-in with Nash had
produced not only the delicious sandwich she had
enjoyed for her lunch but also a very interesting
book written by a local historian, which included
detailed drawings of Hatton at the time it had been
built.

Her mobile started to ring, and as she went to
answer it she recognised Robert's number.

'I'm just leaving London now,' he told her. 'So,
traffic willing, it shouldn't be too long before I reach
you. How are things going? Thanks for your message about the garden ornaments, by the way. I'm

not quite sure what the position is with them. I shall have to check with Nash, but if they are to remain in the gardens then we shall definitely have to take precautions to protect them. Missing me?' he asked her softly then, in a very different tone of voice.

He started to laugh when Faith didn't immediately reply, telling her even more softly, 'You don't have to tell me now. You can *show* me later instead.'

He had rung off before Faith could say anything.

Faith's next encounter with Nash came shortly afterwards, when she went into the kitchen to make herself a cup of coffee. She was just pouring the boiling water onto the coffee grains when the back door opened and Nash walked in.

'Before you say a word,' she told him, 'I bought the coffee myself, and I have the trustees' agreement to use the kitchen,' she added sarcastically. 'Presumably that was a trustees' meeting you were too busy to attend,' she finished, with mock sweetness.

'Faith—' she heard him saying as she turned away from him to return the milk—*her* milk, which she had bought with her own money—to the fridge. Whilst Nash might have taken it upon himself to set the terms for the hostilities between them, she was determined to show him that there was no way she was going to balk at them, or run away in ignominious defeat.

'Perhaps I should ask Robert to mention to them the...difficulties I'm encountering in working here.

Although they have gifted Hatton to the Foundation...' she began.

Faith wasn't used to having to make threats or respond to other people's hostility, but she felt that Nash had left her with little choice.

It comforted her to remember that Nash was not the only trustee of Philip's estate, although she had no real idea who the others were. Whoever they were she certainly had every reason to be grateful to them. Without the extra funds they had made available to her she would never even have been able to consider continuing her studies, as she had done. Nor would she have spent a brief working holiday in Florence—a job which had been organised for her thanks to the very kind offices of one of the trustees, according to her university tutor.

She had had no idea then that Nash was one of their number, and she could well imagine how it must have infuriated him to do anything of benefit for her. But she also knew that he would have adhered scrupulously to the terms of Philip's will. That was the kind of man he was.

'Faith.' Nash stopped her in a grim voice, a voice so determined that it forced her to listen to him.

'I just wanted to tell you that I've put a set of plans of the house in the study for you. They're on Philip's desk.'

Nash was actually speaking to her as though she were a normal human being instead of some loathsome monster. Faith opened her mouth and then closed it again, but the good manners her mother had been so insistent upon forced her to thank him, even though she resented having to do so.

It was much later in the afternoon, whilst she was working on the plans upstairs in her room, that she saw Robert arrive. Putting her work to one side, she went downstairs to meet him.

'Sorry it's taken me so long to get here,' he apologised when they met in the hallway. 'The traffic was appalling.'

'Well, at least you're here now,' Faith offered.

'Mmm…but not for long, I'm afraid,' Robert told her ruefully. 'We're having major problems with the Smethwick House conversion and it looks like I'm going to have to leave you pretty much to your own devices down here until we get them sorted out. Don't look so worried,' he told her with a smile when he saw her expression. 'I have every faith in you.'

He might, but Nash most certainly didn't, and it was Nash she was going to have to deal with on a day-to-day basis, Faith recognised as Robert went on to explain that he had booked a table at a local riverside restaurant.

'We can talk properly over dinner,' he told her, 'but first I need to have a word with Nash. I'm glad he's decided to stay on here for a while. The house is quite remote and I don't like the thought of you being here on your own.'

It was a new experience for Faith to have a man act so protectively towards her. Nash, of course, would have taken a completely different stance, insisting that it was the others who needed protecting from *her*, not the other way around.

After arranging to meet Robert back downstairs in an hour's time, Faith returned to her room to continue with her work.

She began to check the sizes of the upstairs rooms on the plans, noting down those which were large enough to be converted into family-sized rooms and those which were better suited to single occupation.

The downstairs snooker room would, no doubt, be something that the Foundation would want to retain, but she put a question mark over the tennis court, recognising that it might be too expensive to renovate and maintain.

Totally engrossed in what she was doing, Faith was shocked to glance at her watch and realise what time it was. She had barely fifteen minutes left in which to get ready to meet Robert.

Somehow she managed it, snatching a quick shower and changing into a cool black linen dress, and brushing her hair before applying a fresh dusting of make-up.

Despite her blonde hair her skin tanned well, and the hot summer had given it a golden sheen. Her dress, although demure, was sleeveless, revealing the slim tanned warmth of her bare arms and legs.

A bright fuchsia-coloured pashmina which had been an uncharacteristic impulse buy in the sales provided her with a wrap, just in case the evening should prove cool. Faith stroked the silky texture of the wrap gently as she draped it over her shoulders.

Just touching it made her feel very feminine and extravagant. Her mother would have loved it.

She hesitated before opening her jewellery box and putting on the tiny gold-set diamond ear-studs that had been a twenty-first birthday present—and a very unexpected one at that.

She could still remember vividly her shock and speechless delight when she had opened the registered parcel and read the note inside.

'Congratulations on your twenty-first birthday and on the excellence of your academic work', the note attached to the small jeweller's box had read, and instead of any signature there had simply been a typed and very formal, 'The estate of the late Philip Hatton'.

Tears shone briefly in Faith's eyes now as she put the earrings on. That gesture by the anonymous trustees had meant so very much to her, and she could still remember what a thrill it had given her to wear them going out with her university friends to celebrate her birthday.

Robert was waiting in the hallway, smiling admiringly up at her as he watched her descend the stairs.

Although he lacked Nash's arrogantly male brand of sexuality, Robert was a very attractive-looking man—a nice man, Faith acknowledged as she smiled back at him.

'You look good in black,' he complimented her as she reached him. 'It suits you.'

Out of the corner of her eye Faith could see Nash

emerging from the drawing room, and she knew he must have overheard Robert's compliment, even though he chose not to acknowledge either it or her.

She could tell from Robert's behaviour towards her that as yet Nash had said nothing to him about her past, or rather his interpretation of it, but she knew it would only be a matter of time before he did, which meant that she would have to tell Robert herself first. She felt her stomach starting to tense in tight, anxious knots. The shame of what had happened would always cast a dark shadow over her life and she hated the thought of having to resurrect it.

The restaurant Robert took her to was busy and very obviously trendy and expensive. It was the sort of place where private conversation was virtually impossible, and Robert gave her a rueful look as they were escorted to their table.

'I hadn't realised it was going to be as busy as this. I asked Nash to recommend somewhere but I don't think he can have fully understood me.'

Robert's mention of Nash gave Faith the opening she had been looking for. Tentatively she asked him, 'Do you know how much longer Nash intends to remain at Hatton? After all, now that the trustees have handed it over to the Foundation there isn't any real reason for him to be there.'

No reason at all, in fact, other than to torment her, Faith reflected inwardly.

'Well, at the moment the trustees—or rather Nash, should I say, since he is the *sole* trustee of his late godfather's estate— What is it?' Robert asked Faith in concern as she made a small sound of shocked disbelief.

'Nash is the sole Trustee?' she repeated.

'Oh, yes,' Robert confirmed. 'And it was his own idea to get in touch with the Foundation. Apparently he feels very strongly about the needs of children from deprived backgrounds, but, as he's told me himself, he wants to be sure that the Foundation is the right beneficiary for Hatton before fully handing it over. I must admit I'd hate to lose the house at this stage. It's done me no end of good with the rest of the board to be able to say I've secured Hatton for the Foundation.' He gave her a rueful smile. 'Most of them have known me since I was a schoolboy and I'm afraid they still tend to treat me as one.

'I'm looking to you to impress Nash with our plans for converting the house, Faith. I've heard good things about your work and I can well understand why.'

Every word Robert said was adding to Faith's anxiety. How long had Nash been the sole trustee of Philip's estate? she wondered dazedly. Not very long, surely.

'I told Nash of your concern about the garden statues and ornaments, by the way,' Robert was continuing. 'I said you'd told me you were going to make a list of everything. At the moment, like the house and its contents, everything is covered by insurance paid for by the estate, but once Hatton passes legally into our hands that will become the

Foundation's responsibility. I did ask Nash if he had thought of removing some of the more valuable artefacts, but he says he wants them to remain with the house.

'I'm counting on you to do a really first-class job for me here at Hatton, Faith,' Robert repeated. 'An awful lot hinges on our successful acquisition of the house—for both of us. Like I've already said, it will be a real feather in my cap, and I shall make sure that you are suitably rewarded.

'I don't suppose the fact that you and Nash know one another is going to do us any harm either,' he chuckled, so patently oblivious to what Faith was actually feeling and thinking that she felt dangerously close to hysterical laughter as she recognised the weight of the responsibility he was placing on her.

'Robert...I don't think...' she began, carefully and quietly searching for the right words to explain the true situation to him, but he reached across the table gently taking her hand in his and squeezing it.

'Stop worrying,' he told her. 'I *know* you're the right person for the job. After all, I was the one who made the decision to employ you. You can do it, Faith; I know you can. The rest of the board might have thought we should take on someone older— and male—but I know that you're going to prove them wrong and me right.'

Faith's heart sank lower with every word Robert uttered. How *could* she tell him now? How *could* she let him down? She had had no idea that the hand-over of Hatton to the Foundation hadn't fully gone through—or that Robert had had to battle against his co-board members to take her on.

There was only one option left to her now, only one thing she could possibly do—even though it was something that went totally against everything her pride was urging her to do and had been urging her to do for the last twenty-four hours. She was going to have to appeal to Nash, beg him to listen to her for Robert's sake, because of what she felt she owed him for his support of her and for the sake of all those who would benefit from what the Foundation would do with Hatton.

'Not hungry?' Robert asked her solicitously as she pushed her food around her plate.

'I ate a large lunch,' Faith fibbed wanly.

Why was life doing this to her? Why?

CHAPTER FIVE

NASH looked irritably at his watch. Hadn't Faith realised when she had left the house with Robert that, since she didn't possess a set of keys to Hatton, *he* would have to wait for her return before he could lock the house up for the night?

His irritation increased as he recalled the look of male expectancy and desire in Robert's eyes when he had told him during their meeting that he was taking Faith out to dinner.

'There are several things I need to discuss with her, and since we both have to eat we might as well do so together.'

But Nash knew his own sex well enough to know that Robert's real reasons for taking Faith out for a meal were a thousand miles away from practicality—and Faith had obviously had more than business on her mind, as well, to judge from the way she had been dressed when she'd left the house.

The black dress she had been wearing had looked expensive, and the wrap she had draped around her shoulders had had a silky sheen—but not as silky as Faith's softly tanned skin; diamonds had sparkled in her ears...

A bitter, almost tormented look darkened Nash's eyes as he thought about Faith's earrings, but Faith

71

herself would have been stunned if she had known just what was putting that look there.

From the study, where he had been purporting to be 'working' for the last hour, Nash had an excellent view of the darkening driveway that led away from the house to the main road—the driveway down which Faith would have to return.

He had been caught off guard when Robert had brought up the subject of the garden statuary, claiming that Faith was concerned for their security—her concern not just that they could be stolen but also that they could be inadvertently damaged by the children and their parents.

'I have to confess I hadn't realised how valuable and irreplaceable some of the pieces are,' Robert had admitted ruefully. 'And Faith is right. If they are to remain we shall have to find some way of protecting them. We'll need to catalogue them, and then—'

'I already have a list of them,' Nash had informed him brusquely. 'The insurers insist on it.'

Had he misjudged Faith? A stark look darkened Nash's eyes. Here he went again, looking for excuses for her…looking for…

He closed his eyes. Only he knew and only he would ever know just what he had gone through when he had returned home early following a business meeting in London, acting on a hunch…an instinct…something that had felt too urgent to analyse, to discover his godfather lying on the study floor with Faith crouching over him, his wallet in her hands and a look of mixed fury and guilt in her eyes as he'd broken through the circle of girls standing protectively around her to confront her.

Later, as he had waited at the police station whilst Faith and her fellow thieves were being charged—after a two-hour delay since apparently as they were all under age and juveniles they could only be questioned and charged in the presence of a parent or guardian—the police sergeant had commiserated with him and told him not to blame himself.

'These girl thieves—sometimes you'd think butter wouldn't melt in their mouth,' he had offered comfortingly. 'But we see the other side of them, and, believe you me, they can be just as violent and abusive as the lads, if not more so.'

'But my godfather loves Faith,' Nash had protested, still unable to fully take on board what had happened. 'I just can't believe she would do something like this to him.'

What he had really been saying was that he too loved her, and that he couldn't believe she would do something so damaging to *him*, to what he had believed they would one day share—when she was old enough.

'You'd be surprised,' had been the sergeant's dark response. 'Seems from what the others have said that the one who you found holding your godfather's wallet was the ring-leader. She'd put the others up to it. You say she was staying at the house during the summer?'

'Yes,' Nash had agreed numbly. 'She came on a

visit from…from the home, and my godfather invited her to stay. He felt sorry for her. Her
mother…'

The sergeant had sucked in his breath and shaken
his head.

'Got a bad reputation, has that home. There've
been complaints about girls from there stealing from
local shops. They go in a gang—' He'd broken off
as the head of the children's home and the WPC
accompanying her came back into the waiting area.

Unable to stop himself, Nash had hurried towards
them, demanding, almost begging, 'Faith…? Has
she…? Is she…?'

'She still refuses to admit that she was involved,'
the home's head had told him tiredly. 'And I have
to admit I would never have thought… But she is a
very intelligent girl, and sometimes they're the very
ones… They're so much more aware than the others,
you see,' she had added simply. 'They have so much
spare mental energy with nowhere to go.

'She would have seen the opportunities, of course,
when she visited and stayed with your godfather,
and I imagine that the temptation must just have
been too much for her, especially in her circumstances. Her mother has been ill for a very long time
and they have been living in considerable financial
hardship…that often breeds a dangerous form of resentment.'

She had looked down at the floor and then told
Nash uncomfortably, 'She has asked to see you. She
says…' She'd stopped. 'She claims that she is the

victim of the other girls' malice and that she was trying to protect your godfather, not steal from him. But the other girls are adamant that *she* was the one who planned the whole thing, and I have to admit that does make sense.'

'I don't want to see her,' Nash had refused immediately, knowing that he would carry with him for ever, engraved on his mind and his emotions, the scene which had met his eyes when he had walked into Philip's study.

The telephone cord had been cut, but thankfully Nash had had his mobile telephone with him—they had been relatively rare in those days, and he had only decided to buy one himself because, as yet, he hadn't any proper office facilities.

He had rung the emergency services, having first locked the girls and himself in Philip's study. One of them had produced a knife, but he had very quickly removed it from her.

Whilst they had screamed and hurled threats and abuse at him Faith had remained completely silent, and it had only been after the crew had started to carry Philip out to the ambulance and the police had taken charge of the girls that she had finally said anything.

White-faced with terror as she had stared from the police to him, she had begged him to listen, begged him to understand, begged him to believe that she had had nothing to do with what had happened.

'You were holding Philip's wallet,' he had reminded her grimly.

'I was trying to *help* him,' she had protested.

'Don't believe her,' one of the other girls had screamed. '*She's* the one that made us come here…told us it would be easy pickings. She was the one who said the old man was going to be on his own.'

Silently Nash had looked at Faith. Despite all the evidence against her he had desperately wanted to believe that she was innocent, but the look of guilt in her eyes had given her away.

Ignoring her pleading cries to him as the police ushered all of the girls out of the house, he had turned to follow the ambulance crew.

At the hospital they had told him that Philip had suffered a stroke—brought on, they suspected, by shock. He would live, they had assured Nash, but as to how serious the after-effects of his stroke would be they had no way at that stage of saying.

Had Faith shown the slightest degree of remorse, offered him any kind of explanation instead of lying so blatantly to him, he might have given in and agreed to see her. As it was…

'What will happen to her?' he had asked the police sergeant.

'She'll be put in a remand home until they can go before a juvenile court, then it's up to the court to decide what their sentence will be and whether or not it will be custodial.'

Nash had closed his eyes, torn in two by his conflicting emotions. *He* should have been there, with his godfather, to protect him. If he had been…

Bleakly he had turned to leave. He still hadn't been able to believe what Faith had done, and he'd known if he hadn't seen the damning evidence with his own eyes he would *never* have believed it. His godfather had trusted her, loved her...and he himself...

A bitter look had darkened his eyes as he'd made his way to where he had parked his car.

She was fifteen—he had believed her to be naïve and innocent, in need of protection from the desire she had made so obvious she felt for him, from his own increasingly hungry need to respond to it.

How *could* he have been such a fool? She had probably deliberately set out to delude and deceive him right from the start. Physically she was mature for her age; mentally she was as intelligent and knowledgeable, if not more so, as a good many of his own peers.

He had enjoyed their dinner-table debates, enjoyed the passion she brought to every aspect of her life, and he had enjoyed looking forward to the day when the barriers between them could be properly lifted and he could show her just how he wanted and intended to respond to all those sexy, innocent little messages of longing and provocation she had been sending him all summer.

He hadn't just wanted her physically. He had *loved* her, Nash acknowledged grimly now, and her deceit had hurt him, come close to destroying him on just about every level there was.

His godfather's stroke had badly affected Philip's

powers of speech, which he had never fully recovered, and whenever anyone had tried to question him about the incident he had become distressed, saying only, 'Faith... Faith...'

Rather than risk him having a second and even more serious stroke, Nash had insisted that he was not to be questioned any further.

Faith had been lucky to escape a custodial sentence, the authorities had told Nash. That escape had been in the main because it had been her first offence, and because of the plea for clemency that Nash himself had made for her.

Even now he loathed acknowledging that he had been guilty of such a weakness, but the thought of her being sentenced had eaten into him like acid and, despite his anger and contempt, and the bitterness he had felt towards her, he had still interceded on her behalf.

It was what Philip would want, he had told himself, knowing as his godfather slowly struggled to make himself understood that he refused to accept that Faith was in any way to blame, insisting that the other girls had used her...forced her...

Nash had longed to be able to share Philip's belief, but he had known better. He had, after all, seen the guilty expression in Faith's eyes as she'd crouched over his godfather, as well as heard the condemnatory accusations of her co-conspirators.

It hadn't really come as any surprise to Nash when a second and more serious stroke had indeed followed Philip's first one, quickly followed by his death. He still believed that it was the original attack that had caused it—and for what? A paltry few pounds? Because, despite what other people might have believed, Philip had *not* been a wealthy man. He had owned Hatton and its grounds, yes, but a series of bad investments after his retirement had eaten into his capital, and in the latter years of his life it had been Nash who had financed him…who had financed…

He froze as he saw Robert's car heading down the drive.

As Robert brought his car to a halt on Hatton's drive Faith prepared to get out. They had spent longer than she had expected and it was almost midnight.

'I'll see you to the door,' Robert told her, opening his own door.

What Robert had told her had given her a good deal to think about, and her eyes were as shadowed as the garden as she walked towards the house.

'Not so fast,' Robert protested as he hurried to catch up with her and then reached for her hand before Faith realised what he was intending to do.

'I know we haven't known one another very long, Faith, but something tells me that you're a very special person,' Robert murmured, his voice becoming even softer and lower as he repeated huskily, 'A very special person.'

Faith knew instinctively that he was going to kiss her, and as his lips brushed hers with tender warmth, his hands holding her gently, she closed her eyes.

This was how a kiss should be—giving, tender, caring—so why wasn't she feeling anything other than the warmth of Robert's lips against her own? Why wasn't she experiencing the heart-racing, nerve-tightening, stomach-churning intensity of emotion and sensation she had experienced when Nash had kissed her?

Guilty at her own lack of response, she allowed Robert's lips to remain on hers for a few more seconds before gently pulling away.

'Too soon?' Robert asked ruefully, and Faith was glad that the darkness hid the guilt in her eyes as she nodded her head before turning towards the house.

'Don't worry over what I told you tonight,' Robert urged her as he opened the door for her and then stood to one side to allow her to walk past him and go through it.

How could she *not* worry, though? Faith asked herself after she had closed the door behind him. She had once read a book which suggested that an individual was confronted with the same problem over and over again in life, until they found a way of dealing with it.

At fifteen she hadn't been mature enough or strong enough to deal with the harsh realities of the problems Nash had caused her, and now... What was life trying to tell her, to do to her, by making her go to Nash and ask for his clemency?

Faith knew that professionally she was more than capable of doing the job Robert had entrusted her with for the Foundation. In her mind's eye she could already see the faces of the children and their parents when they arrived at Hatton.

Philip had had a very privileged but a very lonely childhood, and she knew how much it would have meant to him to know that this house, *his* house, would be filled with children and giving them so much pleasure. *That* was what must have priority, Faith told herself fervently—the fulfilment of Philip's wishes.

'Fantasising about your lover?'

The unexpected sound of Nash's voice reaching her from the darkness of the moonlit hallway made Faith give an audible gasp.

'Robert *isn't* my lover,' Faith denied unguardedly.

Nash looked away from her as he went to lock the door. He had unwittingly witnessed the kiss Robert and Faith had shared as he'd walked past the study window. There was no doubt in Nash's mind about the role Robert wanted to play in Faith's life—and in her bed—and Faith certainly hadn't been objecting.

As she heard Nash locking the door Faith took a deep breath. There was no point in putting off what she had to do, nor in lying awake half the night worrying about it when Nash was here now.

Before she could lose her courage, she told him quickly, 'Nash, if you've got the time there's something I'd like to discuss with you.'

The slightly nervous, almost conciliatory tone of

her voice, so different from the anger and hostility she had shown him so far, alerted Nash's suspicions.

'It's late,' he told her. 'And I've spent the last hour waiting for you to come back so that I can lock up. Can't whatever it is wait until tomorrow?'

Faith knew that normally such a reaction from anyone, never mind Nash, would have immediately crushed her. But tonight she was so on edge, so uptight and anxious, that she dared not allow herself to hesitate.

'No. I really do need to speak to you now,' she told him.

As she watched him Nash hesitated, and then frowned before striding over to Philip's study and pushing open the door.

'No. Not in there,' Faith refused quickly.

'Where, then?' Nash asked her. 'Your *bedroom*?'

Faith was too overwrought to recognise the sarcasm and bitter cynicism underlying his words, and she certainly had no idea what was going through his mind or what he was feeling. Her one desire was to get her unwanted appeal to him over and done with as quickly as possible.

'Yes, yes…my bedroom is fine,' she agreed almost eagerly, hurrying towards the stairs.

Now what the hell was she up to? Nash wondered cynically as he followed her.

It was Nash's turn to hesitate as Faith pushed open her bedroom door and hurried inside, switching on the light and then turning to confront him as he followed her in and closed the door.

Just for a minute she was tempted to ask him to leave the door open, then mentally reprimanded herself for her foolishness.

At twenty-five she might, for reasons best known to herself, still be a virgin, but there was certainly no need for her to *act* like one.

'Well?' Nash demanded sharply. 'I'm waiting. What is it that's so important it can't wait until tomorrow?'

'Robert told me tonight that it isn't definite yet that the trustees—that *you*,' she forced herself to amend, 'will definitely gift Hatton to the Foundation.'

Nash stared at her, perplexed.

'You brought me up here to tell me *that*?' he asked grimly.

'No,' Faith admitted, bowing her head, unable to bring herself to look at him as she told him in a low voice, 'I hadn't realised it until tonight, but Robert has put himself in a very vulnerable position with the rest of the board by employing me. Apparently I wasn't their choice.'

She stopped and nibbled nervously on her bottom lip.

'I would hate to feel responsible for anything that might jeopardise Robert's position or the Foundation's acquisition of this house.'

For a moment her passionate belief in the work of the Foundation overcame her own anxiety and dread.

'Hatton would be so perfect as one of the

Foundation's homes. I *know* how much it would have meant to Philip to see it put to such a use, and I know too how much it meant to me to be allowed to stay here. I shall always be grateful to Philip.'

'Grateful? You can say that and expect me to believe it after what you did?' Nash demanded gratingly.

Faith's face burned. She itched to defend herself, to throw caution recklessly to the four winds and tell Nash just how wrong he was about her without caring how much such a claim on her part might antagonise him. But of course she could not afford to do that—not now.

Instead she had to content herself with a heartfelt, 'You'll never know how much I regret what happened to Philip, Nash. How much I wish…' She stopped as her throat clogged with emotion. 'Please,' she begged him. 'Please, Nash, we're both adults and we both loved Philip. Surely we can put aside our differences for his sake…for the sake of what he wanted for Hatton?'

'Our *differences*?' Nash threw harshly at her. 'My God, you make it sound as though we've had an idiotic quarrel about some minor incident, not—'

'I do *know* how you feel about me, Nash,' Faith told him quietly. 'I know you feel that I deserve to be punished, even though—' She stopped and made herself focus on the matter in hand, not her own feelings. 'What I wanted to say to you is that if that punishment is going to affect Robert and the Foundation, and Philip's plans for the house, then…'

'Then what?' Nash challenged. 'What will you do then, Faith?'

'Whatever it takes not to have that happen,' Faith told him simply and truthfully. 'I'll do whatever you want, Nash, just so long as you don't stop the Foundation from having Hatton.'

Whatever he wanted! Nash could hardly believe what he had just heard. Faith was offering herself to him in return for his silence.

A furious, savage, destructive anger swept down over him, a culmination of all the years of pain and loss, a dangerous implosion set in motion by the kiss he had witnessed and his own reaction to it.

Years ago she had offered herself to him with what he had then believed to be the innocence of youth—an offer he had truly thought came from love. But he had been so very, very wrong...and only he knew of the nights, the *lifetime* he had lain awake aching for her, wanting her, swearing that he would burn his need for her out of his heart and flesh himself rather than give in to it.

Did she really imagine for a single second that he would take her up on her offer—an offer that proved irrefutably just what kind of person she was? Of course he wasn't going to, not even for the satisfaction of teaching her a much-needed lesson. But he surely had the right to exact *some* payment from her.

'And what does *Robert* think about your...offer... to me?' he asked her silkily.

Faith frowned. Hadn't he been listening to her?

'Robert doesn't know anything about this,' she told him quickly. 'And he mustn't know either.'

Faith was worried that if Robert *did* know he might insist on doing something chivalrous, which might damage his own position, and that was the last thing she wanted.

'So this is to be a personal...*arrangement*...a private agreement?' Nash suggested.

'Yes,' Faith agreed immediately, holding her breath as she waited for Nash to ask her what she intended to do if he didn't agree. Once she had answered that question, informed him that she would hand in her notice rather than prejudice the Foundation's work, she knew there would be no going back. But to her surprise Nash did not ask the question she had been expecting.

As the silence between them grew Faith fiddled nervously with one of her earrings, expelling a sharp sound of distress as it came loose and fell to the floor, dropping down on her hands and knees to look for it.

The images, the temptation, the *torment* of seeing her in such a pose caused Nash to grind his teeth in furious self-denial. How on earth had he *ever* imagined her to be innocent?

As she searched the floor her head was on a level with his groin, the distance between them less than a metre—much less than a metre, he recognised as she crawled closer to him. Totally against his will he could feel his body reacting to her. Angrily he tried to control the fierce upsurge of desire hardening his body, turning away from her as he did so to conceal the evidence of the effect she was having on him.

Suddenly he could see her lying naked in his bed, all silken skin and open arms...

Ten years ago he had dreamed of gently and tenderly initiating her into the pleasure of lovemaking, but now he suspected she could well be the one teaching *him*. Then, at twenty-two, he had considered himself to be reasonably sexually knowledgeable and accomplished, but after he had met Faith—

He had been living in New York the year Faith was twenty-one, dating an 'uptown' woman several years his senior who had made no pretence about her reasons for wanting him in her bed, and *only* in her bed, since she'd had her own very successful career.

They had been planning to have a weekend together out of the city at the Hamptons. She'd had friends who had a house there they could borrow. The day before they had been due to go he had received his yearly report on Faith's progress via the third party through whom he was financing her education, in obedience to his godfather's wishes.

Only he and Philip's bank knew how little money Philip had left, how impossible it would have been to pay for Faith's education out of that money.

The report had been glowingly full of praise for her—not just for her scholastic work but also for the extramural activities she'd been involved in: raising money for children's charities, giving her limited spare time to help teach young children to read. There had even been a mention of her upcoming twenty-first birthday.

To this day Nash had no idea just why he had gone out and bought her those earrings. He had told himself that it was because Philip would have wanted him to do it. Small the diamonds might have been, but they had been the best quality that Tiffany's could supply, set in twenty-four-carat gold. He had mailed them to England before leaving for his weekend at the Hamptons.

His companion had been scornful and vocal about his body's embarrassing failure to respond to her, and although eventually they *had* had sex, sex was all it had been—a joyless, grimly fought for physical coupling which hadn't afforded either of them very much pleasure.

'Oh…thank goodness…' he heard Faith exclaiming now, as her face broke out into a relieved smile and she picked up her earring.

'For God's sake, get up,' Nash commanded. 'I don't need demonstrations of your sexual skills, Faith.'

Her sexual skills! Faith's face burned as she realised just what he meant.

'And as for your *offer*—well, let's just say that the jury is still out, shall we?' Nash told her.

Faith closed her eyes as she stood up. Why on earth had she bothered to try to appeal to him? It was plain that he fully intended to go on tormenting her.

Nash frowned as he heard his own words. What was he saying? There was *no way* he intended to even *consider* the sordid bargain Faith was trying to strike with him.

But something was driving him, savaging him. Something he didn't want to name and couldn't bear to acknowledge.

As Nash turned to walk towards the bedroom door Faith hurried after him. There was something she still had to ask—how long had he been the sole trustee of Philip's estate?

But before she could say anything Nash had turned round, asking her bitingly, 'What is it you want, Faith? This?'

And then he was kissing her, covering her mouth with his, savaging it, destroying the fragile fabric of the illusion she had created for herself that somehow there could be peace between them.

'No!' she tried to deny, reaching out to push him away. But Nash simply swung her round, pressing her up against the door as he cupped her face to prevent her turning away from him.

'Yes,' he reinforced rawly, driving the word into her as he parted her lips with his tongue, thrusting it so powerfully into the vulnerable sensitivity of her mouth that her whole body quivered in shocked recognition of the sensuality of his action.

Imprisoned against the closed door, with the full weight of his lower body resting against her, Faith struggled to combat her own feelings. If Nash's actions had shocked her, then her own reaction to them was even more shocking, and made her even more angry.

Instinctively she knew that never in a thousand lifetimes could Robert make her feel like this, make her experience such a fierce, female clawing and urgent need to match the raw sexuality of Nash's behaviour.

Was *this* the price Nash intended to demand for his silence, his acquiescence to the Foundation's acquisition of Hatton? *Her?* The use of her body in whatever way he chose to use it?

Faith burned with shame and bitter fury—and with another emotion, far stronger than the combined strength of the other two. An emotion that stripped her pride bare and lashed the flesh from her emotions, leaving them raw and bleeding. She *wanted* Nash.

CHAPTER SIX

THE black dress lay in a pool of darkness at Faith's feet and the diamonds she had replaced in her ears shone through the butterscotch and cream of her hair. Her skin gleamed with its own living, breathing warmth, covered only by the nude-coloured cami-sole she was still wearing. But Faith herself was oblivious to the sensuality and torment she presented to Nash. Every hedonistic and wanton urge she had ever possessed was combining with the emotion she had fought so hard to conquer and deny, causing her to cling urgently to him as she returned the fierce passion of his kiss.

It was as though when Nash had released her from her dress he had also released her from her inhibi-tions; the fury and bitterness she had originally felt as he kissed her had burned away to nothing but the sheer power of her response to him.

As a girl she might have dreamed of him kissing her, of them being lovers, but as a girl she had been far too immature to ever dream of anything like *this*—this raw, hungry, aching, overpowering need for him which was filling her, driving her, compel-ling her.

Beneath her fingers she could feel the fabric of his shirt, a barrier to what she really wanted to touch and feel, and she gave a small female growl of thwarted longing, her body tensing with the frustration of not being able to touch him as she so much needed to do, skin to skin, flesh to flesh.

As her fingertips found the opening at the front of his shirt her growl turned to a soft purr of pleasure, but *he* was the one who was trembling from the effect of what she was doing, Nash recognised helplessly as his body reacted immediately to her touch.

He tried to remind himself of why he was here, of why he was doing this, but Faith's fingers were tugging frantically at his shirt buttons and instinctively he started to help her.

'You feel so good...'

Helplessly, totally lost in what she was feeling, Faith moaned the words into his mouth, the movement of her lips against his a series of soft, erotic little flutters that made him shudder from head to toe.

God, but he wanted her...craved her...needed her... He had always known it would be good between them, but had never dreamed it could be like this...

How could just kissing someone make her feel as though her whole body was about to explode? Faith wondered dizzily.

With Nash's help she had finally unfastened his shirt. Greedily she stroked her hands over his naked chest. She wanted to touch him, stroke him, kiss him, lick him, breathe in the pheromone-laden scent of him that was already affecting her so headily.

The only reason he was doing this, Nash told himself, was to remind himself of just what she was, to see just how far she was prepared to go.

Pain streaked the fiery intensity of his longing for her. He couldn't possibly still love her—not knowing what she was, what she'd *done*. But the way she was touching him was driving him crazy…drowning out any kind of logic or reason.

Nash hadn't stopped kissing her from the moment he had pushed her up against the door, Faith recognised giddily. She felt almost drunk, drugged by the way he was making her feel, by the way he was making her need him. Her lips clung to his as the hot, hard weight of his lower body moved against hers, keeping her pinned where she was and reinforcing with every movement how powerfully male he was.

Once, a long time ago, she had broken all the rules, turned her back on convention and, driven by her teenage hormones and her love, had gone to Nash's room, creeping into its darkness to find her way to his bed.

All she had wanted to do was be with him, to have him hold her, love her, but as he had sat bolt upright in the bed she had seen in the silvery light of the moon that he was naked, and a wild, wanton female urge had overtaken her, driving her to beg him to kiss her.

Then, for a moment, she had almost thought that

he might as he had leaned closer to her. She had held her breath and closed her eyes, trembling from head to foot when his hands had closed over her wrists. But the words he had eventually spoken had not been soft, sensual words of love, but a harsh command to her to open her eyes.

When she had complied he had told her firmly, 'This has got to stop, Faith, for both our sakes. You're young and you don't really know what you're asking...or doing,' he had added more gently. 'I promise you that one day you will thank me for sending you away tonight.'

Thank him... Shamed and in despair, Faith had fled from his room to cry herself to sleep in her own bed. But now, as she remembered that incident, she acknowledged that Nash had been right. At fifteen she *had* been too young for the intensity of the raw passion they were now sharing.

Now, she sensed with a surge of erotic female power, there was no way that either of them was going to be able to stop.

Emboldened by her own thoughts, she pulled Nash's shirt free of his jeans.

A long, slow shudder of pleasure rolled through her as she touched his naked torso. But just touching him wasn't enough. She wanted to look at him, taste him, fill her famished senses with the sensual reality of him, with the knowledge that he wanted her, needed her, as powerfully as she did him.

Dragging her mouth away from his was almost a form of torture, but worth the momentary sense of loss it caused her when her awed gaze slid with hedonistic enjoyment over his body.

No film star could ever come anywhere near matching Nash for sheer heart-stopping, hormone-inducing, raw masculine sensuality, Faith decided. He was everything a man could be, everything a man *should* be, and yet, for all the hot, passionate intensity and impatience of her desire, there was still a part of her that was suddenly and sweetly overwhelmed by loving tenderness.

Responding to those emotions, she kissed the top of her finger and gently placed it against the masculine outline of his throat, and then replaced it with her lips, her mouth, slowly starting to kiss her way downwards.

Nash felt as though he had opened a door and walked into his deepest and most private fantasy—only in *that* Faith had interspersed her kisses with words of love.

Ten years old that fantasy might be, but, as he was discovering, it still had the same power over him now as it had done then.

'Faith,' he groaned, taking hold of her and demanding, 'How would you like me to do that to you? To tease you, torment you, lie you down on that bed and slowly kiss my way all over your body?'

As she tilted her head back so that she could look into his eyes Faith knew that her own were betraying her, but she was beyond caring.

'You want that?' Nash was asking her thickly.

'You want me to kiss your breasts, your nipples, your belly...' His voice dropped to a low, raw growl of male arousal. 'That special secret place? Do you want that, Faith?' he demanded. 'Do you want me to kiss you there, to taste you, lick you, make you want to give yourself completely to me?'

Faith couldn't speak. She could barely move; her whole body was held in thrall to the heavy, hot pulse of sensation inside it, that Nash's words had aroused.

Nash couldn't believe what he was saying— thinking...*wanting*... He was like a man possessed, taken over by some alien power—the power of love...

As the words slid into his mind he pushed them away. This had *nothing* to do with love. This was justice. This was—

Faith had started to kiss him, tiny hungry darting kisses that covered his face, his throat, his mouth.

'Take off your clothes, Nash,' she begged him. 'Take me to bed. Show me...teach me...'

Teach *her*! Nash wanted to tell her that he doubted there was anything he could *possibly* teach a woman like her, but she was reaching for the belt on his jeans, fumbling with the clasp, and the feel of those slim feminine fingers fluttering helplessly against his body was doing the kind of things to him that would have brought a stone statue to life.

Even so, he still tried to cling to sanity. He started to say gruffly to her, 'We need—'

But Faith shook her head, interrupting him, telling

him in a desire-laden whisper, 'I need you, Nash. I need you so much…so *badly*…'

Her hand had been resting on his waist as she unfastened his jeans, and now, without him even being aware of her having moved, he felt it sliding inside them. He could feel as well as hear the sound of the aching groan inside his head as her touch grew bolder.

Faith shuddered as the movement of her hand caused Nash's jeans to drop lower and his body to tense. Beneath her fingertips she could feel the crisp thickness of his body hair.

In retaliation Nash slid down the delicate straps of her camisole, exposing the full, taut roundness of her breasts. Her nipples were already hard, responding to the hungry touch of his hands.

As he bent his head, unable to resist responding to the temptation they were offering him, Nash drew a long, shuddering breath. They were behaving like two hormone-crazy teenagers, so hot for one another that they couldn't wait for the comfort of a bed— but they *weren't* teenagers. They were…

The shudder that tormented Faith's body as Nash's lips closed over her nipple drove the ability to think about anything other than what they were sharing completely out of his head. He swept Faith into his arms and carried her over to the bed.

Feeling that she had escaped into the most beautiful dream, Faith watched as Nash removed the rest of his clothes, her eyes soft with love.

As a teenager she had hardly dared to allow herself to imagine being with Nash like this, and as an adult she had closed down that part of herself that was her sexuality. Now those barriers had melted like wax in the heat of the sun, and the sensation that raced and rolled and thrust through her unprepared body as she stared at Nash caused a flutter of such sexually explicit sensation to begin to unfurl, deep inside her, that she gave a small half-shocked, half-bemused little gasp.

'Faith?' Nash questioned her softly, but she shook her head and looked away from him, suddenly as shy and self-conscious as though she had still been fifteen.

Whatever else Faith might lie about she wasn't hiding her desire for him, Nash recognised. But then some women were like that, weren't they? Highly sexed…easily aroused…

Nash leaned forward and kissed Faith's mouth. Her lips clung eagerly to his, her breasts filling his hands, her skin satin-soft.

He kissed her breasts and then her nipples, sucking on them gently, afraid to give way to the full force of his desire in case he hurt her. He kissed the soft warmth of her belly and teased his fingers between the thighs she was keeping unexpectedly tightly closed, moving higher and deeper, feeling her body relax and admit him to the sweet, warm wetness that was waiting for him.

He couldn't wait much longer. Just touching her like this was driving him crazy. In fact, he couldn't wait *any* longer!

'Open your legs,' he whispered to her as he kissed her.

Open her legs! Suddenly Faith felt nervous, afraid of somehow disappointing him. After all, this *was* her first time. She was inexperienced, unknowing.

Hesitantly she started to part her thighs, and then, as Nash started to move slowly over her, against her and then within her, all her doubts and fears fell away and she was climbing, flying, soaring free, a part of Nash as he was a part of her, two equal parts of one perfect whole.

This was what she had been born for, what she had been *destined* for…this and Nash…

As she felt the gathering force of her arousal Faith closed her eyes, Nash's name rising from somewhere deep down inside her, its taste on her tongue unbelievably sweet, its sound on her lips a paean of love and welcome.

Unable to stop herself, she wrapped herself around him and whispered passionately, 'I'm so glad I waited for you, Nash—for this…us… I couldn't have borne it to happen with anyone else…not the first time—' Or any other time, she'd wanted to say, but Nash spoke first.

'What?' he demanded roughly.

She could feel Nash's shock, feel the almost painful momentary cessation of his body moving within hers. The thought of losing him, of losing 'it' now that she was so close, panicked and drove her. Frantically she moved her body against the stillness of his, once, and then again, and again—until with a raw groan Nash was moving with her, for her, carrying them both so swiftly towards the edge of her known universe that Faith could only cling on to him desperately as the feeling engulfed her, sweeping her into its own vortex.

As he heard Faith cry out Nash shuddered, caught up in the undertow of the sharply conflicting emotions savaging him.

Faith had been a virgin! That was impossible…unbelievable… But his body knew differently, had somehow sensed the truth about her even before she had told him herself. But where his mind had registered the danger of what he was doing once he had heard the words, his body had reacted very differently. And even before Faith herself had so recklessly urged him on he had known that he couldn't control his body's desire for her.

Nash closed his eyes and then opened them again, moving away from Faith as he got off the bed and started to reach for his clothes.

Faith's virginity altered none of his feelings about what she had done to his godfather. How could it? He had no idea why she hadn't had any previous lovers—although he did know it couldn't have been from any lack of offers. Had she been saving it until she met the right man? A man rich enough to give her the lifestyle she wanted? A man such as Robert Ferndown?

If so, then why throw away such a valuable bargaining counter now, and with him?

To buy his silence? A long shudder ripped through him. Did she *really* think…?

It no longer mattered what she thought, or what he felt. How could it? What mattered now was what they had done.

'What is it? Why are you going?' Faith demanded anxiously as Nash pulled on his clothes. *Why* was he leaving her when he should be holding her, loving her?

Her body felt weak; she was in both physical and emotional shock, unable to comprehend anything other than the fact that Nash was deserting her.

Nash waited until he had reached her bedroom door before asking his question.

'Why?' he demanded emotionlessly. 'You're twenty-five, Faith, a woman.'

What was he trying to say—that she was too old to be a virgin, that he wished she had not been?

Faith felt as though someone had cut her emotional veins and she was slowly bleeding to death, slowly growing colder and colder, emptier and emptier of the love that had burned so hotly and fiercely in Nash's arms. Ten years apart from him hadn't been enough to destroy it and neither had the accusations he had flung at her or his misjudgement of her. No, she had had to wait for now, in his *arms*, to have her love destroyed, murdered, as he had so often accused her of murdering his godfather.

From somewhere she managed to find enough pride to respond stiffly to him.

'It wasn't a conscious choice.' She gave a small,

careless shrug and a bitter little smile. 'I'm sorry if it wasn't what you were expecting—'

Nash stopped her savagely. 'You should have *told* me.'

'I did...' Faith reminded him quietly.

'Not *then*. My God... *That* was too late, Faith,' he grated, underlining his meaning and adding crudely, 'By the time you told me I doubt that a chastity belt could have stopped me!'

'*I* wasn't the one—' Faith began defensively, but immediately Nash stopped her again.

'*You* were the one who offered me sex in return for my...silence,' he told her sharply. 'You're un-believable—do you know that? What were you thinking? That I'd stop and that your virginity—your prize bargaining counter—would remain in-tact? Was *that* why you pretended to be so eager to touch me, Faith—because you were planning to make sure that things never got as far as penetration, that I wouldn't be able to last that long?'

Faith listened to him in disbelief. She had *never* offered him sex. What was he *talking* about? And as for the rest of what he had said—a deep, angry tide of colour swept over her.

'I suppose it's too much to hope that you're using some form of birth control?' Nash continued wea-rily.

One look at Faith's face confirmed his worst fears.

Faith could feel herself starting to shiver. Now, with her body empty of the sensual urgency and need which had driven her, she couldn't understand how she had behaved in the way she had. As she forced herself to meet the hard, angry topaz glitter of Nash's gaze her own fell away.

'I…I can't be pregnant,' she began to stammer, 'Not after just the once…'

The sound of Nash's laughter shocked her even more than his rejection of her.

'I don't *believe* this,' she heard Nash saying forcefully. 'And from you, the girl your tutors praised to the skies for your maturity and intelligence…your sense of responsibility, your compassion for other people.'

'You read my tutors' reports?' Faith's forehead began to pleat in suspicion.

'They were with your references for the job,' Nash told her after a brief pause. 'Not that *that* matters now,' he added dismissively. '*Now* you and I have rather more urgent things to worry about—don't we?'

Red-faced, Faith turned away from him. He was right, of course he was right, and she didn't know why she was behaving so stupidly.

As he opened her bedroom door Nash hesitated.

'Does Ferndown know about…your virginity?' he asked her abruptly.

The hot colour in Faith's face became a burning wave of anger.

'What business is that of yours?' she began, biting her lip as she saw the look Nash was giving her. 'No! No, he doesn't,' she admitted reluctantly.

CHAPTER SEVEN

IT WAS five o'clock in the afternoon. Faith hadn't seen Nash in nearly two days—since that night when he had left her bedroom, in actual fact—and for some reason the emptiness of the large house was now beginning to prey on her a little—the emptiness of the house or the absence of Nash?

The former, of course, Faith insisted firmly to herself as she tried to return her concentration to her work.

Yesterday morning when she had come downstairs to find a note in the kitchen from Nash, saying that he had gone away 'on business', her immediate reaction had been one of overwhelming relief.

What had happened between them that night was something she wanted to seal up and hide away somewhere, with a large 'Danger—do not open' label on it.

Absent-mindedly she started to doodle on her notepad, a horrified expression widening her eyes as she saw the entwined hearts symbol she had drawn.

What was the matter with her? She didn't love Nash—not any more—and he most certainly did not love *her*. But she had…

Her face burning, she stood up and walked over to the study window. It was being here at Hatton that was the cause of her problems and responsible for what had happened—being here at Hatton with *Nash*. Only Nash wasn't here now, so she ought to be able to concentrate on her work instead of...

Had Nash really left 'on business', or had he left because he wanted to put some distance between them, to underline to her that he didn't want her in his life?

Faith tensed as the study door opened, her heart thumping, but it was only Mrs Jenson the house-keeper.

'I'm off now,' she told Faith.

As she tried to smile in acknowledgement Faith was sharply conscious of the other woman's unspo-ken hostility towards her. She had sensed it the first time they had met, and she didn't think it was just her imagination that it had become somehow more brazenly threatening in Nash's absence.

Hadn't she got enough problems to contend with without worrying about Mrs Jenson? Faith asked herself as the housekeeper turned to leave, and re-turned her attention to her work.

Whilst she worked she tried to visualise Hatton in its converted state, but worryingly such a vision refused to form for her. Instead the only person she could see living here at Hatton was Nash.

The only person?

Agitatedly Faith turned round. Surely it was only natural that when she visualised Nash she should also visualise a family, *his* family, with him? she tried to defend herself.

Maybe. But was it also natural that she should visualise that same family—those two little girls, those two strong-jawed boys—with Nash's unmistakable topaz eyes and her own Scandinavian hair colouring?

It was just her memory playing tricks on her, Faith insisted with inward mental indignity. It was just because once, a long time ago, when she had been too naïve and silly to know better, she had fantasised that one day she and Nash would have such a family. It meant nothing now. *Nothing*…

Her eyes clouded as reality forced her to acknowledge an anxiety she had been pushing to the back of her mind.

Lost, deep in thrall to the wonder of making love with Nash, irresponsibly she had not given a single thought to what the result of that lovemaking might be. Without a previous sex life there had been no need for her to consider such things.

She *couldn't* be pregnant, she tried to reassure herself. Apart from anything else she was well past the age when something like an accidental pregnancy was allowable. She was a woman, responsible for her own life—and for a new life which she and Nash might have created?

Her mobile rang, interrupting her thoughts, and the sound of Robert's voice made her uncomfortably aware of just how what had happened with Nash was likely to be viewed by other people—and especially Robert himself.

'I just thought I'd ring to see how things are going,' he explained.

Quickly and professionally Faith outlined to him what she was doing.

Was the business Nash had left to conduct anything to do with the Foundation and the house? Faith did not feel that it was her place to ask, and Robert already sounded harassed and preoccupied.

'How's the Smethwick contract going?' Faith asked him.

'Not very well,' he admitted. 'I'm having lunch with the other members of the board tomorrow and I suspect I'm going to be asked to come up with a solution to the delay. I don't suppose Nash has said anything to you about Hatton?' he asked Faith hopefully.

Faith was still feeling guilty about Robert and the problems he was having later in the evening as she cleared away her supper things and then made her way back to the study.

They were having a wonderful spell of good weather and she was tempted to spend the evening outside in the garden. But she had run into a problem with her work on the conversion of the house which she wanted to get to grips with.

Large as it was, in terms of a family house, Faith was concerned that the costs involved in its conversion to a respite home would be too high in relation to the number of people it would ultimately be able to house.

The wonderful Jekyll gardens were not designed for children to play in, and to destroy them in order to create something that was suitable seemed almost sacrilege.

Faith was still trying to find an acceptable solution to the problem several hours later, when Nash arrived back.

As she saw him getting out of his car her first inclination was to hide herself away in her room; her face was already starting to burn a self-conscious pink. But her life had given Faith both courage and the determination to stand up for herself. Why *should* she hide herself away? What had happened between them had, after all, taken two, even if...

She discovered that she was holding her breath as Nash opened the front door.

She had left the study door slightly ajar; surely he would guess from the fact that she had the light on that she was working here, even if he had not seen her from the drive. And he would, of course, be as reluctant to see her as she was him.

Faith heard the breath rattle betrayingly in her lungs as Nash disproved her anxious theorising by pushing open the study door and walking in.

In the dark-coloured business suit he was wearing he looked even more dauntingly and overpoweringly male.

The remembered torrid heat of their lovemaking seemed to engulf Faith as she tried to match the subtle domination of his body language.

'I know it's late but there's something we need

to discuss,' he told her brusquely as he pushed something towards her across the desk.

'What's this?' Faith asked him uncertainly, eyeing the piece of paper uneasily. She had no idea what it was, but the look on Nash's face was enough to set all her own internal alarm bells clanging.

'It's a special licence,' Nash told her grimly.

'A what?' Bemusedly she looked at him.

'A special licence,' Nash repeated in a clipped voice, adding before she could say anything, 'I know the bishop—he was a close friend of my father's—and he agreed exceptionally to grant us a licence to get married. I've made all the arrangements. The service will take place tomorrow morning at eleven. I've already seen the vicar. He was—'

'Married?' Faith interrupted him in a shocked voice. 'No! *No!* We can't! That's not possible,' she objected. Her heart was pounding. She felt dizzy…disbelieving…filled with panic and yet somehow distanced from what was happening, as though she was merely an onlooker watching her own emotions, observing her own reactions.

But Nash was speaking once again, telling her sharply, 'I'm afraid it isn't merely possible, Faith, it's essential. You and I *have* to get married. We don't have any other option.'

Faith could feel other emotions beginning to filter through the protection of her shock now: painful, hurting, damaging emotions that were almost too much for her to bear. Emotions she couldn't allow herself to even acknowledge, never mind examine.

'Why?' she asked Nash, her voice high with defensive panic. 'We don't—'

'Do you *really* need to ask me that?' Nash cut across her with grim cynicism. 'You could be pregnant.'

Faith closed her eyes and took a deep steadying breath. No, of course, she didn't.

'Are you trying to suggest that we should get married because of a baby I may or may not be carrying?' she questioned him sharply.

'Because you may be carrying *my* baby,' Nash agreed harshly, 'and because...' He walked over to the study window, keeping his back towards her as he told her coldly, 'No matter what my opinion of you might be, Faith, I have my own moral code. An old-fashioned moral code by modern standards, perhaps, but it was Philip's code, and in many ways he had more of an influence on my childhood than either of my parents.'

He paused and then turned round, catching Faith off guard so that there was no time for her to conceal the pain she knew must be in her eyes as he continued mercilessly, 'Had you been more...experienced...'

'You're saying we have to marry because I was a *virgin*?' Faith demanded, her disbelief colouring her voice. 'But that's...that's archaic, Nash.'

'To *you*, I dare say it is. But the fact remains that according to *my* moral laws it is the right thing, the *only* thing I can now do.'

Faith took a deep breath.

'And if I refuse?' she asked him, holding her head high as she forced herself to challenge his control of what was happening.

'I can't allow you to do that, Faith,' Nash told her sombrely, maintaining the kind of blistering eye contact with her that would normally have left her raw with pain and despair. 'If it helps to sweeten the pill for you just try reminding yourself that you've played the bargaining counter of your virginity extremely well, and that *my* wealth is far in excess of Ferndown's—although I dare say I shall keep a much tighter hold on it where you're concerned than he would.'

Faith couldn't speak. She couldn't think; she couldn't even breathe so deep and traumatising was what Nash had said to her.

She was, she discovered vaguely, trembling... shaking. Not with fear but with anger...temper... rage...fury...pride...that Nash should dare to speak to her as he had. But somehow she managed to control the desire to give vent to her feelings and instead to say, as calmly as she could, 'There may not be a child.'

The look he gave her was as vitriolic as pure acid.

'Because it was your first time?' he derided her, watching in grim satisfaction as her face flooded with colour. 'As I've just told you,' he continued coldly, 'that is *not* the whole issue.'

'Yes, I know. You're doing this because I was a virgin,' Faith repeated flatly. She couldn't keep the furious disbelief out of her voice. 'Nash, that's...

that's—' She stopped, unable to find the words to convey her feelings to him. 'What if I *wasn't* really a virgin? What if you just thought that I was?' she challenged.

'You're getting hysterical,' Nash told her dismissingly. 'Overreacting…'

'*I'm* overreacting?' Faith exploded. Why was she bothering arguing with him when it was plain that he had made up his mind and that he wasn't going to change it?

Well, she didn't have to go along with his plans…his orders. She was a free agent. She could walk out of this room, get into her car and…

'Don't even think about it,' she heard Nash advise her warningly, somehow managing to place himself between her and the door, as though he had read her mind. 'Tomorrow morning you and I are getting married,' Nash repeated. 'And whatever has to be done to achieve that *will* be done.' He gave a small brief shrug. 'I'm surprised you're making such a fuss. After all, you're getting what you've already proved you want.'

His words, uttered with such a careless lack of compassion, caused Faith to feel as though her heart was being squeezed in a giant vice.

Had he guessed, then? Had she *shown*…? Did he dare to think that just because she had been foolish enough to give in to her desire for him she was still idiotic enough to harbour her teenage infatuation for him? Did he even, perhaps, think that she'd still been a virgin because of him...because of wanting him...loving him?

Faith opened her mouth to tell him furiously that he was wrong and then closed it again, her body going weak with relief as he added, 'You wanted to marry for money, Faith, and that's exactly what you are doing.'

Money. Nash thought... Shakily she closed her eyes, too caught up in her own feelings to deny Nash's insulting insinuation.

'Oh, and just in case you *should* try to do anything stupid, perhaps I should warn you now that until we are married I shan't be letting you out of my sight.'

'Until... But that means...' she began to protest, and then stopped.

'Yes?' Nash encouraged her.

'We aren't going to get married until tomorrow. What are you planning to do, Nash? Sit up all night outside my bedroom door to make sure I don't escape?'

Faith realised the moment she looked at him in the silence that followed that she had dangerously overreached herself in attempting to challenge him.

'*Outside* your bedroom door?' The look he gave her was pure purgatory. 'Don't be naïve, Faith. Since we've already anticipated our marriage vows there's precious little point in us not sharing the same bed, and it will certainly make it easier for me to ensure that you don't do anything...foolish...'

'By what?' Faith challenged him furiously, 'Handcuffing me to—?'

She stopped as Nash purred dangerously, 'Don't tempt me. Is bondage something you like to fantasise about, Faith?' he asked her shockingly.

'No,' Faith denied immediately.

'No? So you don't like the idea of emotionally enslaving a man...of making him long for your love. Bondage needn't be just physical,' he added tauntingly.

'I don't like the idea of any relationship where the two people in it don't meet as equals,' Faith managed to find the courage to tell him. She couldn't believe that any of this was really happening. That Nash really intended they should marry, for the most idiotic, impossibly antiquated reasons she had ever heard.

And by special licence—like two desperate lovers whose greatest need was to be together.

Well, she was certainly going to feel and look the most unbride-like bride the local vicar had ever married, she told herself defeatedly, considering the workman-like clothes she had brought to Hatton with her.

If it had been anyone other than Nash who had proposed such an impossible alliance she would have argued and fought to get them to change their mind. But, as she had good cause to know, once Nash had adopted a position, an attitude, a *judgement*, nothing and no one could shift him from it.

'You can't possibly want this marriage,' she protested in one final attempt to persuade him to see reason.

'This has nothing to do with what I *want*,' he retaliated immediately. 'It's what I *have* to do.'

'But we don't love one another, and if there's no child…' Faith protested.

'You'll what?' Nash asked cynically, misunderstanding her question. 'Take a lover? If you do, Faith, you'd better make sure that he really wants you and that he can afford you, because I shan't tolerate any unfaithful wife—and with our past history…'

Their glances met and clashed, but to her intense fury and chagrin Faith discovered that hers was the first to fall away.

Nervously Faith pulled the bedclothes up to her chin and lay facing the bedroom door. She had taken two of the herbal sleeping tablets she occasionally used and was praying that she would be fast asleep before Nash carried out his threat to join her.

She had no chance of escaping. Nash's car was blocking her own in and he had the keys to the house. A tiny inner voice warned Faith that she wasn't making as much attempt to escape as she should, but she dismissed it as illogical and unhelpful.

What was she supposed to do—jump out of her bedroom window?

And besides, if she *should* be pregnant… She had grown up without her father and, even worse, she had seen at first hand how much her mother had missed having the support of the man she loved. The husband and the father who had not been there had cast a shadow over both their lives.

Her tablets were beginning to take effect. Faith could feel her thoughts slowing down, her eyelids growing heavy. Tomorrow she was going to marry Nash. A soft tremor ran through her body. Nash... His name was on her lips as she finally slid into sleep.

Downstairs Nash stood motionless in front of the study window, looking out into the now dark garden.

He knew that to a lot of people—no doubt to Faith herself, included—what he was doing would seem old-fashioned and unnecessary. But Nash believed in taking his responsibilities seriously, and what could be more of a responsibility to a man than the knowledge that he could have fathered a child?

It had shocked him and caught him more off guard than he liked to acknowledge to discover that he was Faith's first lover. If he closed his eyes he could even now visualise her as she had been at fifteen. But it had been a woman he had held in his arms two nights ago, a woman he had made love with.

A woman who had not previously activated her sexual self and yet, for some reason, had chosen to do so with him. *Him*—the very last man she might logically have chosen. Why?

Irritably he turned away from the window. When had there ever been a logical reason for what Faith chose to do? She had kept her virginity to use as a bargaining counter—and then thrown it away on him.

Perhaps, like him, she had found herself in a situation over which she had had no control. Perhaps, like him, she too...

She too what? Explosively he cursed under his breath and frowned as he caught sight of his brief-case. He had brought it in with him from the car. Almost reluctantly he opened it and removed a small file from it, taking out the papers inside and spreading them out on Philip's desk.

The contents of the reports from Faith's tutors were so familiar to him he could almost have quoted them verbatim. She'd been a hard-working, dedicated scholar, determined to do her best. 'A young woman with integrity as well as intelligence', was what one of her tutors had written about her.

How easily she had deceived them. As easily as she had deceived his godfather... Nash's glance fell on a separate piece of paper. Frowning, he reached for it.

It was a letter which Faith had written to the trustees shortly after she had been informed of Philip's bequest. In it she expressed her surprise and gratitude and made a promise that she would do everything in her power to repay Philip's faith in her—'You cannot know how much it means to me to know that Philip believed in me and in my innocence…'

Her *innocence*! If only she *had* been innocent.

She had *known* of his concern for Philip's health. He had talked to her about it only days before she and her little gang had broken into the house, his anxiety having caused him to drop his guard and confide in her. And in doing so had he unwittingly been as instrumental in what had happened to Philip as she had been herself?

She had *known* that he was going to be away from the house and that Philip would be on his own. He had told her so himself. And she had known too of the older man's increasing frailty. There had been certain little warnings. Philip had complained on a couple of earlier occasions about a 'weakness' in his arm—a classic sign that he might even then have been suffering from very minor strokes, according to his doctor.

What had Philip thought when he had first seen her…when he had first let her in? He would have been pleased to see her, delighted by her unexpected visit, Nash knew. How many times had he tormented, tortured himself, imagining what Philip must have gone through when he had finally realised the truth? That Faith's visit had not been motivated by love but by greed. And for what? Philip had never kept more than a hundred pounds in cash in the house—never!

A hundred pounds.

Nash could still remember his godfather's solicitor's bewilderment when Nash had told him what he intended to do.

'You want to pay for this young woman's education and you want her to believe the money has come from your late godfather's estate?'

He had been bemused…perplexed, dubious even, but Nash had been insistent—and insistent, too, that Faith was to believe that her inheritance was being handled by several anonymous 'trustees'.

At first it had given him a certain grim sort of pleasure to know that he had so much control over her life…her future…to know that, if he should so choose, with one word he could destroy her. He could take away from her the golden opportunity she had been given. And while Philip's death and his own feelings of guilt about it were still raw, Nash had needed that kind of savage mental satisfaction.

Later, as the reports had started to come in from her tutors, praising Faith not just for her dedication to her work but also for the way she herself was as a person, his feelings had changed, veering between contempt and anger that she should so easily deceive them and a dark, bitter sense of loss.

His own weakness towards her had infuriated him then and still did now. Why the hell couldn't he accept what she was instead of wishing…wanting…? What if she *was* carrying his child? How was he going to protect that child from the disillusionment of knowing what his or her mother was?

He didn't know, but somehow he would have to find a way.

Picking the papers up from the desk, he replaced them in the folder and locked it in his briefcase. He took it out to his car and opened the boot, placing it inside and at the same time removing the other contents of the boot: a large hat box embossed discreetly with the name of a very expensive milliner, a dress bag bearing the name of an even more expensive designer, plus a box containing a pair of shoes with heels so high and spindly they had made his eyebrows arch. But the exclusive store's personal shopper had been insistent and so he had given in.

After carrying them back into the house he locked the door and then took them upstairs.

When he walked into her bedroom he saw that Faith was sleeping with all the innocence of a young girl.

Putting the packages down on the floor, he left the room.

Downstairs in Philip's study he poured himself a glass of whisky, lifting it to his mouth and then putting it down again untasted. *That* wasn't going to solve his problems.

Faith woke up abruptly. Last night she had forgotten to close her curtains and now the sun was shining in. Nervously she turned her head, but to her relief the other side of the bed was empty, its pillow undented. And then she saw the packages on the bedroom floor.

What on earth...?

Pushing back the bedclothes, she slid out of the bed and padded towards them.

She opened the shoebox first, her eyes widening as she saw the delicate cream satin stilettoes. They were in her size, though she would never have bought anything so fragile nor so expensive. She turned to the hat box, holding her breath as she eased off the lid. She had to remove several layers of tissue paper before she could lift out the hat.

Disbelievingly she stared at it. Cream, like the shoes, it was a froth of fine straw and raw silk. A wedding hat. Her heart slammed heavily against her ribs. Very carefully she restored it to its box. Her hands were shaking and she had to blink several times. Not because she was crying. No. The only tears she was likely to shed today would be tears of rage and resentment—and not because Nash had touched her emotions. How on earth could he? How on earth could she be foolish enough to let him?

She stared at the dress bag for several minutes before she could bring herself to unzip it.

The dress and coat inside it were also cream— exactly the right shade for her particular colouring and the right kind of style for her build. At the bottom of the dress bag was a small cache of tissue-wrapped items—underwear and sheer hold-up stockings. Nothing, it seemed, had been forgotten. Nothing overlooked to equip her for her role of bride.

For a moment Faith was tempted to bundle the

whole lot up and fling them out of her bedroom window. How *dared* Nash do this? How *dared* he make a mockery of everything that a wedding day should be? How *dared* he compel her into making meaningless vows for a marriage that was a desecration of everything that love should rightfully be?

It was early, not even seven o'clock yet. Quickly she showered and then pulled on her own clothes— a soft cotton top, jeans—slipped her bare feet into her shoes.

They were going to have another hot day.

The hat, the dress and the shoes were all back in their original containers. It was a struggle for her to carry them all but somehow she managed it.

Nash was sleeping in the same room he had always used. Faith was so angry that she didn't even bother to knock warningly on the door, simply thrusting it open and marching in, going over to the bed, where she dropped everything carelessly onto it, and at the same time announcing furiously, 'You may be able to force me to marry you, Nash, but there's no way that you can force me to do so wearing…wearing *these*.'

Nash was sitting up in his bed, his face darkening.

'So what *are* you going to wear?' he asked her sarcastically. 'Your jeans?'

'I'm not a child or a doll, to be dressed up to…to suit your whims,' Faith exploded.

Behind her anger lay tears, and the sharp, despairing misery she was determined she was not going to allow Nash to see. Her wedding outfit was something she should have chosen herself, with excitement and pride and joy and love. Not…not something Nash had felt obliged to buy because he knew she wouldn't have anything suitable in her wardrobe. And if he had really loved her it wouldn't have mattered to either of them what she wore when they exchanged their vows, because all that would matter would be their shared love.

Their *shared* love? She *didn't* love Nash.

'I'm not wearing that outfit, Nash,' she reiterated.

'No? Then what will you do when our son or daughter asks to see our wedding photographs?'

Wedding photographs! What photographs? Faith wanted to challenge him, but irresistibly she had a mental image of the child Nash had conjured to life with his words. Their child…Nash's daughter or son—and hers.

A hot, sweet, dangerously yearning feeling spread through her, transfixing her.

'I've brought you your tea, Mr Nash, and the papers. Oh—'

Faith could feel the heat burning her skin as the housekeeper came into the room. The knowing smirk she was giving them made Faith cringe. There was something about the woman that she really did not like. It made her feel not just acutely uncomfortable but somehow vulnerable as well. It was obvious that Nash, though, did not share her feelings, nor her embarrassment. 'Thank you, Mrs Jenson,' he greeted the housekeeper. 'You can be the first to congratulate us. Faith and I are getting married this morning—aren't we, darling?' he added, and he leaned forward and took hold of Faith's hand, drawing her down towards him before Faith could stop him, his mouth brushing with deliberate slowness against her own.

The speculation in the other woman's eyes as she sidled towards the door was almost more than Faith could bear.

'*Why* did you have to tell *her*,' Faith asked Nash angrily as soon as she had gone.

'Would you have preferred her to think we were just having sex and to spread it all over the village? You may not care very much about *your* reputation, Faith, but I can assure you that I care a great deal about mine.'

'I now pronounce you man and wife...'

Faith was shaking from head to foot, tiny shudders of tension and emotion running seismically through her body.

The sunlight through the stained glass windows of the old Norman church glinted on the rings she was wearing—a single solitaire diamond of breath-taking clarity that somehow reminded her of her earrings, and a matching plain gold band. They were married. She was Nash's wife.

Nash's *wife*! Another deeper shudder shook her.

All those years ago when she had fantasised about marrying Nash she had never imagined she would do so feeling like this.

She was wearing the clothes Nash had bought for

her. Not because of anything Nash had said but because in the end she had felt that the vicar of a small country church might find it offensive that she should choose to be married in jeans and a tee shirt. It had been for his sake, out of respect for his feelings and for the church itself, that she had changed her clothes.

'I can't remember the last time I married a couple by special licence,' the vicar was saying, and Faith could tell from his voice that he believed he had just married a couple who were desperately in love.

Desperately in love! Once that had been *exactly* how she had felt about Nash.

Once!

Certain memories of the way she had responded to Nash in bed, the way she had felt about him, refused to go away.

But that didn't mean that she still loved him, she tried to reassure herself, fighting against her inner panic. How *could* she after what he had done?

The atmosphere inside the church was one of peace and timelessness, a quiet, gentle benediction. A sense of the faith of the people who had worshipped here for so many generations touched her soul, Faith recognised as she paused to draw strength from her surroundings.

No marriage should ever be entered into like this, in mutual distrust and hostility.

She couldn't bring herself to look at Nash as they left the church together.

CHAPTER EIGHT

'I'LL be off then, now. I've finished upstairs. Wednesday is always my day for upstairs, although it's taken me longer than usual seeing as I've had the *two* beds to change.'

Faith frowned as she heard the mocking note underlining the housekeeper's words, but she refused to let the older woman see that she had recognised it.

No doubt it *would* seem odd to her that a newly married couple should sleep not just in separate beds but in separate rooms.

She grimaced to herself as she remembered the furiously angry words she had flung at Nash on the day of their marriage.

'I might have to share a life with you from now on, Nash, but there's *no way* ever we will share a bed.'

'Then it's just as well I wasn't planning to invite you to do so, isn't it?' Nash had returned after the briefest of pauses.

'No. You've already *done* what you wanted to do, haven't you?' Faith had lashed out at him, driven by a sense of desperation and pain she'd been unable to control.

'If you're trying to insinuate by that comment that

126

I knew you were a virgin and that I deliberately—'
Nash had begun dangerously, before stopping and
shaking his head.

'We're married now, Faith,' he had told her flatly,
'which means that there's hardly any point in trying
to provoke me into changing my mind, is there?'

'But we *will* be having separate rooms, won't
we?' she had insisted stubbornly, holding her breath
as she'd waited for him to argue with her.

Only he hadn't. Instead he had simply shrugged
his shoulders dismissively and responded, 'If that's
what you want.'

Of course it was what she wanted... It had been
then and it still was now—wasn't it?

It was probably only her pride that was making
her feel so...so somehow lacking as a woman just
because of Mrs Jenson's smirked comment. Anyway, Faith had far more to worry about than the
housekeeper's views on her marriage.

Far more!

It was a hot, sultry day and Faith was tempted to
blame the heat for the problems she was having in
trying to concentrate on her work. Another few days,
no more than a week at most, and she should know
if the night she and Nash had spent together was
going to result in a child.

Instinctively she glanced down at her left hand.
Her rings were slightly loose, and she twisted her
diamond solitaire 'engagement' ring absently.

'Why have you given me this?' she had challenged Nash as he had driven back to Hatton from the church.

'They came as a pair,' he had responded with a dismissive shrug.

A pair…

She and Nash were now a pair, in the eyes of the rest of the world and the law.

She had tried to ring Robert earlier in the week to tell him that she and Nash were married but had been told by his secretary that he was up in Scotland visiting an elderly cousin who had been taken ill.

'He's asked me to hold everything but the most urgent messages,' she had informed Faith.

Helplessly Faith looked at the plans she was supposed to be working on. No matter how hard she tried she just couldn't get properly motivated. Every time she started to make practical notes on how the house could best be adapted to suit the Foundation's needs she started to visualise Philip showing her around it, the pride in his eyes as he had done so.

Abandoning her work, Faith went upstairs and removed her tee shirt, tying on a brief halter-necked top before going outside into the garden. Nash was away on business and she had the house to herself. Absent-mindedly she bent down to remove a weed from the long border.

Half an hour later there was a growing pile of weeds next to her on the gravel path and she was diligently occupied in adding to it.

The sky had taken on a brassy hue and the air

had become heavy. The weather was forecast to break later in the week, bringing much needed rain.

Nash frowned as he walked into the empty study. There was no sign of Faith in the house but her car was parked outside.

His frown deepened as he scrutinised the plans she had been working on. They were for the ground floor of the house and he could see from her notes that she was concerned that the existing kitchen facilities would not be adequate for the Foundation's needs.

She had done a small but detailed plan, showing how some of the house's larger rooms could be divided to provide the facilities the Foundation would need. Nash reached out to turn them over and tensed as he saw the plans Faith had put beneath them.

These were very different from the ones she had been working on. They showed the ground floor of Hatton very much as it still was, but with the addition of a pretty conservatory and the alteration of the old butler's pantry and scullery area next to the kitchen to provide a large airy family room. Nash studied what she had done for a long time before sliding the top drawing back over it.

The deal he had been putting together in New York was a complex one but it was finally getting close to completion, Nash thought, then paused as he reached the top of the stairs, glancing out of the window that looked out onto the garden. He could see Faith busily weeding. Her brief halter top exposed the smooth tanned flesh of her back. She had tied her hair up out of the way.

It had been a long flight from New York and it had been his intention to have a shower and go straight to bed—so why was he turning round and heading back down the stairs?

Faith didn't know just what it was that made her stop what she was doing and turn her head to look down the long walkway. Some sixth sense? Some instinct? The instinct of a woman for a certain man?

Her heart slammed against her ribs as she saw Nash. He had taken a shortcut from the house to the walkway and was standing just in front of the small gazebo which commanded a view of the entire length of it. A little unsteadily Faith got to her feet.

The air was so oppressive and heavy that it seemed to physically press in on her, and the sun had disappeared, swallowed up by a warning bank of heavy cloud which was slowly darkening the sky.

Faith gave a small shiver as she saw it. It was the kind of sky that presaged thunder. She knew her fear of thunderstorms was illogical, but that didn't stop her dreading them.

Nash watched her as she stood irresolutely glancing from him to the sky. Once she would have run to him, her face lighting up with joy at the sight of him as she flung herself into his arms. Here, in this very gazebo, she had clung to him, lifting her mouth temptingly towards his as she'd told him, 'Oh, Nash…I'm so glad you're back. I've missed you.'

The kiss he had given her had been just the merest

brush of his mouth against her cheek, unlike the one he had *wanted* to give her, plundering the soft sweetness of the lips she was offering him, cupping her face, stroking the silky softness of her throat, removing from her body the thin top she had been wearing and slowly caressing her breasts, watching the pleasure shine brilliantly in her eyes as he did so before whispering to her how much he loved and wanted her.

Grimly he pushed aside his unwanted memories and walked towards Faith.

Why was he looking at her like that? Faith wondered warily. Was he thinking that she ought to be inside working and not out here? She flinched as she heard a faint roll of thunder in the distance.

Nash heard it too. Faith, he remembered, was terrified of thunderstorms. Irritably he pushed away his feeling of relief that he had reached Hatton before the storm. Why the hell should he feel any need or desire to protect her?

'I think I'll go back inside,' Faith told him, her eyes on the darkening horizon.

Her hair was starting to come loose and she reached up to remove the band she had secured it with, unintentionally unfastening the tie on her halter top at the same time. Her concentration was more on the growing storm than on what she was doing.

It was only when she felt her top starting to slide free of her body that she realised what she had done, and held it protectively against her breasts with her hand. With the straps tangled in her now loose hair, discreetly retying them wasn't going to be possible—and anyway it was obvious from the way Nash was looking at her that he realised what had happened.

'I applaud your modesty, but is it really necessary?' he asked her dryly. 'Women sunbathe topless openly in public, Faith, and it would be a very secluded person these days who isn't familiar with the sight of naked female breasts. And besides...' He stopped, but Faith knew what he had been going to say.

He had been about to remind her that he was no stranger to her naked body—and not merely the sight of it either!

He had been walking alongside her, but now he was standing behind her, one hand lightly touching her naked shoulder as he told her, 'Keep still for a minute and I'll refasten it for you.'

It was a mundane enough remark, and a mundane enough action, surely—merely tying two pieces of cloth together, that was all. But as he refastened her straps his fingers brushed against her skin, sending messages that were far too dangerously sensual shooting through her. Her body felt too sensitive, too aware of him. She could feel the frantic race of her heartbeat, driven by a mixture of fear and pain, and her tension was exacerbated by the distant slow roll of the still thankfully distant storm.

What if Nash were to bend his head now and gently kiss the slope of her shoulder before turning her round to face him? Beneath her top Faith felt her nipples harden, whilst a hot coil of desire began to tighten deeper within her body.

If things were different between them wouldn't *she* now be turning to *him*, smiling teasingly up at him whilst she silently invited him to kiss her, touch her…make love with her…?

Why was she thinking like this? Had Mrs Jenson's comment to her earlier affected her more than she had thought? Had it somehow challenged her as a woman to such an extent that she felt she had something to prove?

'There…'

'Thank you.' Her voice was curt, her body screaming with tension. Why was Nash still holding on to her? She could feel his breath against her skin, so warm, so close that it was almost as though he was whispering the softest of kisses against her naked shoulder. Frantically Faith fought to remind herself of the reality of her situation. If she did have something to prove, surely that something was that she was in no danger whatsoever of succumbing to her teenage feelings for Nash?

The thick sulphurous silence of the garden was so oppressive that even the bees had gone silent.

'Have you told Ferndown yet?'

Nash had released her as he spoke and automatically Faith spun round to face him.

'If you mean have I told him about…that… that…about our marriage,' she answered, 'Then, no…I haven't.'

'Faith—' Nash began, and then stopped as a low, growling roll of thunder made her flinch.

'We'd better get inside. With any luck the storm will bypass us here,' he told Faith as they hurried towards the house. 'My solicitor's coming out to see me later. Otherwise—' He stopped speaking, his mouth suddenly grim.

Otherwise what? Nash asked himself with inward scorn. Otherwise he'd stay with her, protect her, hold her...take care of her?

As Faith lifted her hand to pull open the house door the diamond in her engagement ring caught the light and glinted brilliantly. He had ordered it specially from Tiffany's, and he had lied when he'd said that it was part of a matching set.

Once she was inside the house Faith felt less afraid. She couldn't hear the storm now. It was, mercifully, still too far away.

Faith started up nervously from her chair as she heard the unmistakable sound of thunder. It was ten o'clock in the evening and she was on her own in the house watching television—or rather trying to—in an attempt to distract herself from what was happening outside. The local weather forecast had predicted that the storm would pass them by, but the increasingly loud claps of thunder Faith could hear above the noise of the television didn't sound as though it was doing any such thing.

Nash had taken his solicitor out to dinner. She had been invited to join them, but of course she had refused. She had seen the curiosity in the older man's eyes when Nash had introduced her to him as his wife.

Why had Nash had to do that? She had felt such a hypocrite accepting his good wishes. His late cousin had been Philip's solicitor, he had informed Faith.

And so, of course, he would know about Philip's bequest to *her*, for which she owed such a debt of gratitude.

Another roll of thunder shook the sky. Unable to stop herself, Faith rushed to the window and opened the curtains. The storm had brought an early murky dusk, and as she peered out anxiously into it a jagged fork of lightning splintered across the sky.

The storm was in the distance and she had nothing to fear, she knew. It would bypass the house. But she just wished it would hurry up and do so.

She had been caught in a bad thunderstorm as a small child and she suspected that that was the original cause of her now almost phobic fear of thunder. Her desire to run and hide was totally illogical, she told herself firmly as she forced herself to leave the window and go back to her chair.

If she turned the television up loudly enough she wouldn't even hear the thunder, and anyway it would soon be gone—except that half an hour later Faith knew that it wasn't going away. It was coming closer and closer.

In the restaurant in Oxford where he had taken his solicitor Nash broke into the older man's fond reminiscences of Philip.

'I'm sorry,' he apologised, 'but I'm going to have to go. Faith is terrified of thunderstorms, and contrary to the forecast this one seems to be moving closer to us.'

They had travelled to Oxford in separate cars since David Lincoln lived on the other side of the city, and within minutes of calling for the bill Nash was back in his own car and speeding towards Hatton.

Switching on the radio, he heard that the storm had changed direction and that it was proving to be worse than the original forecast.

Frowning, Nash put his foot down on the accelerator. It was only natural that he should be concerned, he told himself. After all, Faith could be carrying his child.

But as fast as he drove, the storm was faster. He could see it illuminating the sky in front of him, hear its savage ferocity, and he knew from the time lag between the vivid pyrotechnics of the lightning and the threatening rolls of thunder that the centre of the storm was still some miles away.

Another jagged flash of lightning tore open the sky before it earthed.

Nash cursed as minutes later his car headlights picked out the tree it had hit, the huge branch now blocking the road.

Quickly reversing his car, he drove back the way he had come. The only alternative route he could take was a circuitous one that would add well over another half an hour to his journey.

He glanced at his dashboard clock...

Faith trembled as another bolt of lightning exploded in the darkness outside her bedroom window. Anxiously she started to count, waiting for the follow-up burst of thunder.

Ten seconds...twenty... The storm was miles away yet—miles away.

She was perfectly safe. There was no need for her to panic. Hatton had withstood nearly a hundred years of summer storms.

But it was built on the highest piece of land locally; its tall, decorative chimneys reached up into the sky. The fury of the storm left Faith in no doubt about its need to find an escape...a prey to vent its pent-up energy upon. Around her bedroom window was the frame which had once held the metal bars that all nursery windows of a certain era had been fixed with. If the lightning should find and strike it...

As though in some malign way it had read her thoughts, a sudden vivid flash of lightning illuminated her bedroom window.

Faith could feel her fear overwhelming her as fast as the storm was threatening to overwhelm the house.

There had been a storm the summer she had stayed here. Nash had found her crouched on the landing, her hands over her ears. He had taken her to his room, talking to her, soothing her, staying with her until the storm had passed.

Nash!

Faith screamed his name as the thunder crashed and rolled outside, drowning out the sound of her terror. She was a creature of the elements now, incapable of any kind of logic, driven by instinct and fear.

Wrenching open her door, she raced along the landing, her breath coming in painful rasping sobs as she finally reached Nash's bedroom. The room was in darkness, a silent stronghold of peace and safety, somehow inviolate from the storm.

In here she would be safe, Faith knew instinctively. As she closed the door she could hear the storm raging ever closer.

Shaking with the nauseous intensity of her fear, she crawled into Nash's bed, wrapping the bedcovers tightly around herself.

'Come on,' Nash had urged her gently all those years ago when the storm had finally died away. 'It's gone now. You can go back to your own bed.'

'I don't want to go,' Faith had protested. 'I want to stay here with you.'

And she had clung to him as she spoke, silently willing him to let her stay. Against her ear she had heard his heartbeat, accelerating as she moved, and her own heart had lurched yearningly against her ribs as she'd prayed that he would let her stay, let her show him how much she loved him, how grown up she was...how ready to be his.

But instead he had shaken his head and told her firmly, 'You *can't* stay here, Faith—you know that...'

And then, before she'd been able to say another word, he had picked her up in his arms and carried her back to her room and her own bed, for all the world as though she was still a little girl and not the fully grown woman she had wanted him to see her as.

Another crash of thunder engulfed the house, blotting out even the sound of her own scream. Frantically Faith reached for Nash's pillow, pulling it over her head.

Safe beneath its darkness as the thunder momentarily abated, she realised that the pillow carried Nash's scent.

As she breathed it in a huge wave of feeling rolled over her. Tears filled her eyes. Things could have been so very different between them if only Nash had believed her, trusted her, loved her. Her mind stepped back to the night that had destroyed her dreams...

She had visited Hatton the previous weekend and Nash had told her that he was going away. It had simply never occurred to her that there was a hidden agenda behind the questions she had been asked at school about whether or not Nash would be there.

'No,' she had replied, never dreaming what was being planned. It had only been by chance that she had actually found out. Another girl who had overheard a snippet of conversation had alerted her to what was going on.

It was three miles from the home to Hatton, and she had run all the way, arriving with a stitch in her side, terrified that she might be too late to warn Philip of what was going to happen.

The front door had been open—evidence, it had been claimed later, that *she* had been the one to organise everything and that Philip had unsuspectingly let her in. She had heard voices coming from Philip's study. When she had rushed in she had found Philip collapsed on the floor with the gang ransacking his desk and, most sickeningly of all, one of them standing over him, holding his wallet.

Frantic with shock and anguish, Faith had gone to protect Philip, getting between him and his attacker and snatching his wallet out of her hand as she'd done so. And it had been whilst she had been crouching protectively beside him that Nash had arrived.

At first she had been too relieved to see him to realise what interpretation he was putting on the situation.

Even when the ringleader of the gang had deliberately lied to him, claiming that she, Faith, was the one responsible, the one who had organised their break-in, it had never dawned on her that Nash would believe it.

The ambulance and the police had arrived together, and Faith had become almost hysterical with shock and disbelief when she had realised that, far from being allowed to go in the ambulance with Philip, she was going to be taken to the police station with the rest of the gang.

Once there she had pleaded to be allowed to see Nash—so sure even then that she would be able to make him see the truth, so sure that there had to have been a mistake, that it would be totally impossible for him to believe that she would do *anything* to hurt Philip.

But Nash had refused to see her, refused to believe her.

Virtually overnight she had grown up, become the woman she had so much wanted to be—and that woman had made a vow to herself that the love she had felt for Nash was going to be totally destroyed, ripped out of her...

Faith gave a gasp as the whole house seemed to reverberate with the intensity of the thunder, bringing her back to the present and reality. She was too terrified now to scream, too terrified to do anything but lie frozen with fear in Nash's bed, her only source of comfort and strength his familiar scent.

Nash cursed as he opened Hatton's front door. The storm was virtually overhead now, and it was, as the reporter on the local radio station had just said, the worst to strike the area in over twenty years.

Calling out Faith's name, Nash checked Philip's study and then the kitchen, before racing up the stairs two at a time. Her car was outside so he knew

she was in the house, and he guessed that she would
have taken refuge in her bedroom.

The door to it was open but the room itself was
empty. The bedclothes were half on the bed and half
off it, indicating that Faith had, at some stage, gone
to bed. But where was she now?

No light shone beneath the door of the bathroom
but Nash checked it anyway, still calling her name.
Fear of the kind he knew Faith suffered allied to a
storm as bad as the one they were having was a
dangerous combination. If she had panicked and
perhaps run outside she might have fallen, be lying
somewhere terrified…hurt… It was pitch black outside, and as he'd come in it had started to rain.

'Faith…?' No reply.

Had she been panicked into leaving the house?
There was a flashlight in his car but he would need
a more protective coat.

As he reached his bedroom and realised that the
door to it was open Nash felt his heart lurch against
his chest wall.

Ten years ago, in the middle of a summer storm,
Faith had sought refuge with him in his room. But
things had been different then. His room was the
last place she would go now in search of sanctuary
and safety—wasn't it?

Hardly daring to breathe he stood still, his breath
leaking from his lungs in a long, slow, painful rasp
as he saw the almost impossibly small bump she
made in the middle of his bed.

She had curled herself up so tightly that her outline beneath the bedclothes was almost that of a child.

As his eyes accustomed themselves to the darkness of the room he saw his pillow and the way she was clutching it tightly to her, her face buried beneath it.

The storm had reached its crescendo: lightning so intense that it actually hurt his eyes to see it, followed almost immediately by a burst of thunder so loud that even Nash himself winced.

The small tight bundle that was Faith shook so much the whole bed shook with her.

Pity and an emotion far too dangerous for him to name arced through him.

Sitting down on the bed, Nash reached for her.

At first Faith thought she was dreaming, that in fact she had actually been killed by the thunderbolt and that she was now in a place where dreams, fantasies, somehow came true. How else could she be here in Nash's arms whilst he tenderly wrapped his bedding around her shivering body, at the same time telling her that she was safe and that there was nothing to worry about because the storm would soon be over?

'No, don't look,' she heard him commanding her as she stared towards the window and saw the greedy darting flicker of lightning, as quick and as deadly as a serpent's tongue.

Overhead the thunder still pounded the house, but Nash was gently pushing her head into the curve of his shoulder, holding her, his actions unbelievably tender and more than distracting enough to take her mind off what was happening outside.

'The storm will soon be gone,' he was telling her again soothingly, his arms tightening around her as she flinched against another roll of thunder.

Ten minutes later, with the sound of the rain outside louder than that of the dying growl of the thunder, Faith tried to persuade herself that he was right.

'I would have been here sooner but there was a tree across the road,' Nash was telling her.

He had thought about her…come back because of *her*?

The warm Nash smell enveloping her was so much stronger when it came from Nash himself, and its almost magical ability to comfort her was making her reluctant to move away from him. The very thought of going back to her room, where she knew she would lie awake all night dreading the return of the storm, made her shake inside with anxiety.

All those years ago when the storm had died away Nash had insisted on returning her to her room. Now Faith could feel him starting to move away from her.

'No.' She clutched immediately at his sleeve. 'Don't make me go back go my own room, Nash,' she begged him. 'The storm might come back.'

'You want to stay *here*?'

It was too dark for her to see his expression but she could hear the sombreness in his voice.

Under more normal circumstances pride would have driven and dictated her answer, but there was no room for pride inside her now.

'I want to stay here,' she admitted, taking a deep shuddering breath before adding, 'And I want to stay with you. I want to stay here with you, Nash,' she reinforced, as though she was afraid he might not understand her need. 'Just until the storm's gone,' she whispered. 'Just for tonight.'

As he exhaled slowly and carefully into the darkness above her downbent head, with the soft warm weight of her in his arms, Nash gave in.

'Just for tonight,' he agreed huskily.

CHAPTER NINE

'YOU won't go to sleep and...and leave me awake on my own—will you?'

Faith's anxious question reached Nash across the darkness that separated them, her little-girl nervousness tugging at his heartstrings. He had managed to persuade her to relinquish his pillow and to allow him to go to her room to get two more, but by some unfortunate mischance whilst he'd been gone the storm had made a dying rally, returning to shake the sky, and he had found her virtually paralysed with terror as she crouched on the bed.

The discovery that she was naked beneath the bedclothes she was holding in a death-like grip had made him wish he had thought to bring more than just her pillows from her room, but when he tried to move away from her to go back she refused to let him go, clinging to his arm with the fingers he had gently removed from the bedding.

'I have to get undressed, Faith,' he told her ruefully. 'I need a shower and a shave.'

He saw her head turn in the direction of his *en suite* bathroom.

'If it makes you feel any better you can come with me,' he offered teasingly, trying to distract her from her fear.

Reluctantly she let him go.

'You won't be long, will you?' she urged him as he headed for his bathroom.

'No. I shan't be long,' he assured her.

Like her, it was his habit to sleep naked. But tonight... A little grimly he wrapped a towel around his lower body before heading back into the bedroom.

Faith was exactly where he had left her.

Now, lying in the same bed with her, so close to him that he could feel her breathing as well as hear it, Nash wondered wryly if she had *any* idea just how unlikely it was that he would be able to sleep. Perhaps it was as well that she didn't!

The storm had gone, leaving the air cooler and fresher. Faith stretched sinuously, luxuriating in the pleasurable warmth of the large bed and her body's awareness of the protective presence of Nash. A sleepy, sensual and wholly womanly smile curled Faith's mouth as her relaxed senses responded to the knowledge of Nash's proximity.

Instinctively Faith snuggled closer to him, her hand curling possessively round his arm, the breath leaving her lungs on a long sigh as her lips nuzzled the warm flesh of his throat.

In her half-asleep state it was easy for Faith to abandon the barriers she had put up against her feelings and allow her deepest and most sensual self to have its way.

This was Nash as she had so much longed for

him to be all those years ago, and subconsciously her body registered that fact, pouring through her veins a soothing reality-diffusing elixir that was a mixture of emotion and desire and one other very powerful ingredient which her deepest self knew and recognised.

'Mmm…'

As she stroked the bare skin of his arm and gently tasted the warmth of his throat with her half-open lips her whole body was washed with a sweetly languorous wave of female pleasure.

'Mmm…'

Faith moved even closer, her body touching Nash's as her fingertips gently explored him.

Nash had barely slept, unable to snatch more than a few seconds of rest before forcing himself back awake just in case… Just in case what?

Certainly not just in case Faith started doing what she was doing right now. *No*… What he had been afraid of was that *he* might be tempted to…

After the accusations she had flung at him on their wedding day he had told himself that he would never allow himself to be tempted to touch her again, no matter how much he might want to do so. Lovemaking wasn't something he wanted to feel he was forcing on her—it was something that should be shared, like love itself.

He tried to grit his teeth against the raw moan of pleasure her touch was commanding.

Helpless to stop his body's reaction to the stroke of her gently explorative fingertips, he did the only other thing he could, reaching out and taking hold of her arm, lifting her hand away from his body. As he did so the naked warmth of her breasts brushed against his skin.

A long, slow uncontrollable shudder of reaction ripped through him, the groan he was unable to silence causing Faith to open her eyes.

She was in bed with Nash! Wonderingly she gazed at him, her eyes soft with emotion, her body still far too powerfully affected by the hormones his proximity had released to listen to any cautionary warnings of her mind.

Had she any idea just how powerfully sensual the way she was looking at him was? Nash wondered despairingly as he felt his self-control melt beneath its heat.

'Nash.'

As she whispered his name Faith leaned forward, her lips parting in a deliberate and irresistible invitation to be kissed. When he hesitated, the look in Faith's eyes deepened and darkened, and she moved even closer to him, the top half of her body resting on his as she brushed his mouth with hers.

A virgin she might have been, but when it came to tempting a man she most definitely knew how to be all woman, Nash acknowledged as he closed his arms around her and opened his mouth over hers.

Faith felt as though she might melt from the sheer intensity of the heat engulfing her as Nash kissed her.

His eyes, like hers, were open, focusing on her,

hypnotising her into a state of physical and emotional responsiveness that totally swept away her inhibitions.

She might be completely awake now, mentally completely aware of what reality was, but her body was still lost in the sensual spell that this night-long proximity to Nash had woven around it.

'Nash...'

As he lifted his mouth from hers she raised her hand and gently touched his lips. His body moved against her. One of them was shaking. It had to be her. She felt as though she was sinking, drowning in the depths of Nash's gaze.

His lips caressed her fingertips, his tongue-tip stroking each one individually before his fingers curled around her wrist and his mouth moved downwards into her palm, making her quiver, then along her arm, lingering on the sensual spot just inside her elbow and making her tremble almost violently as his touch generated a response that threatened to devour her.

She could feel it right down to her toes, all the way up her spine to where the tiny hairs at the nape of her neck were lifting in a sensual signal as old as time itself.

In the shadowy light she could see the pale curve of her breast and the darkly flushed tensely aroused peak of her nipple, already aching with its need to feel the erotic suckle of Nash's mouth.

Beneath the bedclothes her belly tightened, her hips moving, lifting as she pressed herself closer...

closer; and an almost violent spasm of pleasure racked her as she felt the hard, hot pressure of Nash's arousal.

And all they had done was kiss…just once… And she wanted more…all of his kisses…all of him…

Nash tried reminding himself of all the reasons why he should not give in, but his mind was listening to a very different kind of argument, one that said she was his, they were married, this was his destiny—this and whatever might result from their intimacy—and that the debt of responsibility he would owe the child they might conceive would outrank the debt of responsibility he owed his godfather.

They might conceive? But it was too late for his brain to issue an urgent warning, his body, his heart, his *soul*, were already in thrall to a far more elemental urgency.

Faith felt as though she finally understood what it was to experience ecstasy, to reach a place that made her feel immortal and, even more awe-inspiring, made her feel that she and Nash were finally meeting as equals.

There were no more barriers between them. They weren't just touching naked flesh to naked flesh, but naked soul to naked soul. And instinctively, immediately, she knew, in the very heartbeat of time, that it had happened. She felt the fierce, final surge of Nash's desire within her, carrying her forward to her own sharp high plateau of infinite pleasure, and knew that this time they *had* created a new life.

Nash couldn't sleep. Anger, guilt, despair and a helpless longing for things to be different denied him the peace that Faith was enjoying.

Like her, he had been sharply aware of the soul-baring intimacy of what they had shared. Like her, too, a part of him had experienced the awesomeness of the beating wings of destiny hovering over them. But now that moment had gone he was once again facing the same emotion-churning dilemma he had faced so many times before. He was still unable to reconcile what he felt for Faith in terms of his love for her with what he knew cerebrally he ought to feel—because of what she had done.

If he allowed himself to love Faith he would end up hating himself. If he forced himself to hate her he would—

Restlessly he got out of bed. All his adult life he had made his own decisions and stuck to them. Now, though, he acknowledged that he needed help. Now he needed the wisdom and compassion that had been Philip's.

He showered and dressed, leaving the house whilst Faith still slept. He needed to be on his own to wrestle with his own demons. Being with Faith distracted him too much, made it impossible for him to think of anything other than how much he loved her.

There! *Finally* he had admitted it, allowed himself to acknowledge it…to face it…

No matter how much guilt or anguish it cost him to accept it, his desire for Faith, his love for her, was no different now than it had been before her cruelly heartless attack on Philip.

Conscience, logic, pride might insist that he should feel differently, that he should loathe her for what she had done and despise himself for wishing he could find some way of excusing her, but they all weighed as feathers in the scales that tipped so heavily in favour of his love for her. A love that might be weighted with sorrow and guilt, but a love he couldn't ignore or defy.

In his bed, holding her, responding to the sweet sensuality of her, he had seen the woman he'd always believed the girl he had known would become. All sweet, wanton allure laced with uninhibited passion, and yet somehow, at the same time, touched with an innocence and an honesty that made him ache with love for her.

She was a mystery, a conundrum, a question he could find no logical answer for. It was as though in hurting his godfather she had somehow stepped totally outside her own character and behaved in a way that was alien to her true nature.

Grimly he mocked himself for his own thoughts as he got into his car and started the engine.

Philip was buried near Oxford, in the peace and tranquillity of the small graveyard of the church where his parents had been married, and where they were also buried. As he drove there Nash remembered how he had half-hoped, half-dreaded that Faith would come to Philip's funeral, only learning later that her mother had died virtually at the same time as Philip.

He remembered too how that first year he had missed the anniversary of Philip's death, returning from New York several days later to find that some-one else had visited the grave ahead of him, that that someone had planted it with Philip's favourite flowers and left a bunch of scented roses which had just begun to fade.

He had known who they were from even before he had read Faith's message.

To Philip in remembrance.
Dearly loved and dearly missed. Your faith in me has lightened my darkness and your inspiration will guide me all my life.
Faith.

Nash rubbed his hand across his eyes as he re-membered the tears he had shed. Tears of anger and self-denial, tears that had burned his eyes like acid rather than washing them free of pain.

Her duplicity had infuriated him, and he had been sorely tempted to seek her out and tell her just *who* was paying for her precious education, just *who* she had to thank for the second chance at life she had been given. But of course he had done no such thing.

An eye for an eye, a tooth for a tooth, and a heart for a heart? Did Faith have a heart? Nash wished he knew.

*   *   *

A little nervously Faith emerged from her own bed-room and headed for the stairs. She had woken up an hour ago, her body so sensually relaxed that she had immediately blushed with self-consciousness as she'd remembered just *why* it felt that way.

At first she had assumed that Nash was in his bathroom, but when he had not emerged she had managed to pluck up the courage to leave his bed and check for herself.

She had no idea just why he was allowing her the privacy to come to terms with what she had done, but she was supremely grateful that he was. Faith was not going to try to deceive herself. *She* had been the one to institute their...intimacy. *She* had been the one to turn to Nash, to touch him, to kiss him...to...to...

Her face was well and truly on fire now. She tried desperately to think rationally. But what was reason or logic when her body was still languorous and hedonistically relaxed with pleasure and her heart was overflowing with the most intense kind of emotion?

She and Nash had made love. Made *love*. Not merely had sex. They had made love as they had surely been destined to do, and just as soon as she could Faith was going to sit him down and *make* him listen to her whilst she explained to him just what had happened that fateful night. This time somehow she would *have* to find a way to make him accept. Because... A little self-consciously her hand covered her stomach, but there was delight and joy in the smile that curled her mouth as she drew in and then expelled a shaky breath of awareness.

This wasn't just something she was doing for herself because she was finally prepared to admit that she still loved Nash, she told herself determinedly. It was something she *had* to do for the sake of the child she was so sure they had conceived. They owed it to their child to give him or her not just their individual love but also their *shared* love.

Their *shared* love? Strong-mindedly Faith refused to allow herself to even suspect that Nash *didn't* share her feelings. Surely after what they had experienced together he *must*.

Instinctively she felt for her rings and then frowned. She was wearing her wedding ring but where was her 'engagement' ring? Had she taken it off last night during the storm without realising what she was doing?

She was halfway down the stairs when she heard the front doorbell. The sight of Nash's solicitor standing outside momentarily disconcerted her, but she made him comfortable in Philip's office before going in search of Nash—only realising when she did so that Nash's car was missing.

'It doesn't matter,' David Lincoln assured her. 'I just wanted to return some papers to him. He forgot them last night.' He smiled at Faith. 'He was very anxious to get back to you.'

His skin pinkened a little. 'So very romantic, and what one might describe as a perfect ending. I have to confess when he first told me what he intended to do all those years ago I was a trifle uncertain—but, Nash being Nash, he was insistent. "It was Philip's wish that Faith should complete her education," Nash told me, and he fully intended to make that possible despite the fact that there just wasn't the money in Philip's estate to allow for such a bequest.

'Of course you'll know all about that now,' he told Faith warmly. 'I must confess I was never really sure just why Nash was so insistent that his involvement was to be kept a secret, or why he wanted you to believe that several trustees were administering your bequest when in fact Nash was the only one—paying for your education out of his own pocket.'

Stunned, Faith let him continue to sing Nash's praises.

Nash had paid for her to go to university, not Philip. *Nash* had supported her during the years she had been studying, learning. Nash…

A horrid feeling of nauseous light-headedness engulfed her, a sense of shock and disbelief; a sharp coldness was replacing the delicious warmth she had woken up with. Nash *owned* her. Nash had *bought* her…and last night he had no doubt simply been claiming his repayment.

An icy wave of desolation and loss swept over her. She felt as though something infinitely precious had been taken away from her, although it took her several minutes to analyse what it was.

What had made Philip's gift so very special to her had been her belief that it proved he had known her innocence. But now… Had Philip even *wanted* to help her, or had that too simply been another lie created by Nash?

As he parked his car outside Hatton's front door Nash took a deep breath. Had the hard-won peace and purposefulness he had felt as he knelt beside Philip's grave deserted him or was it still there? Had he finally laid the past to rest and accepted that if he wanted to move on he must draw a line under the events leading up to Philip's death?

He loved Faith, no matter what she was. He knew that. He knew too that as a girl she had loved him. And, earlier, in his arms he had felt…*she* had felt… But in order to give those feelings a chance he had to put aside his own bitterness and guilt.

Today, kneeling on the soft earth in the churchyard, he had felt somehow that Philip was giving him his blessing, urging him to build a new life for himself and for Faith as well. And for the first time since it had happened Nash actually felt able to admit to his own feelings of guilt at not being there when Philip had most needed him—guilt he had previously offloaded onto Faith. Whether or not they could turn their relationship around he didn't know, but what he did know was that they needed to talk.

Faith had seen him arrive, and she was waiting for him when he walked into the hallway.

'I want to talk to you—'

'We need to talk—'

Both of them spoke at once, and then both of them stopped.

'Will Philip's study be all right?'

Faith heard and recognised the unexpected, almost tender tone to Nash's voice, and just for a second her resolve wavered. Perhaps she had misunderstood.

Nash was already ushering her into Philip's study, his hand remaining in the small of her waist as he paused to close the door, almost as though he couldn't bear to totally relinquish his physical contact with her.

She didn't wait for Nash to finish closing the door before she burst into speech, demanding sharply, 'Is it true that *you* financed me through university, Nash? That there *was* no bequest from Philip?'

Nash frowned as she hurled her angry questions at him like missiles flung heedlessly in a furious attack. Her anger was as mystifying to him as the cause of her questions.

'What makes you think—?' he began, but Faith cut him short.

'Your solicitor was here. He told me. He seemed to think that this—' she held up her left hand, showing him her ring finger, her voice filling with contempt '—is the culmination of some romantic fantasy between us. If only he knew the truth. The only reason you would ever pursue me is for revenge.

'Is that why you did it, Nash? Out of some perverted desire to exert control over me, to buy my future so that you could hold the power to destroy both it and me if you chose?'

Faith knew that her voice was becoming wilder and wilder, like her claims, as her imagination tormented her with increasingly shocking motives for what Nash had done.

'It was Philip's wish that you were given the chance to fulfil your ambitions,' Nash told her quietly, once he had had time to realise what had happened.

'He *told* you that, did he?' Faith demanded bitterly. 'He *said* he wanted you to pay for me to—?'

'No,' Nash was forced to admit. 'He wanted to do something to help you. He had it written into his will...' Nash stopped and looked away. 'Unfortunately in the end he wasn't able...either physically or financially...to make the provisions he wished to make.'

'So *you* made them for him,' Faith persisted fiercely. 'Why?' she demanded sharply. '*Why* did you do it, Nash? *Was* it because you wanted to have some kind of hold over me? To be in a position to go on punishing me for Philip's death?'

The accuracy of the accusations she was hurling at him startled Nash, and shocked him too. Hearing his own emotions put into words gave them a rawness, a blind cruelty and lack of charity that left a bitter taste in his mouth. Was it too late for him to plead with her for understanding and clemency, or would she respond to him in the same way he had once responded to her when she had pleaded with him for those very same things?

How often through the years had that knowledge haunted him…that *regret*? But how could he explain to her now and expect her to understand that he had refused to see her simply because he had been so afraid that he might weaken, because he had believed so passionately that he owed it to his godfather not to do so.

As she waited for his response Faith twisted her wedding ring round her finger.

Broodingly Nash focused on it, and as she recognised what he was doing Faith went still. Nash was looking at her hands, her rings. Only she wasn't wearing her engagement ring because she hadn't been able to find it as yet. Her engagement ring—with its uncanny similarity to the earrings Philip's 'trustees' had given to her to mark her twenty-first birthday…the earrings she had valued and treasured with such joy and love.

Anger and betrayal flooded her in equal measure.

'*You* bought my earrings,' she told Nash. '*You*…'

Nash winced as he heard the bitterness and loathing in her voice.

'It was what Philip would have wanted me to do,' he told her, just as he had always told himself.

'How *could* you?' Faith demanded in a raw whisper. 'How *could* you do something like that and yet at the same time still believe that I was responsible for Philip's death? Can you even begin to *imagine* how it makes me feel? Knowing that everything I am I owe to you. My education, my qualifications, Florence, my job!'

'You got your job on your own merits, Faith.'

'No,' she denied. 'I got it on your money. Your money and the education it bought for me. Have you *any* idea how much I hate knowing that, Nash? How much I *hate* knowing that everything I am I owe to your charity? Is that what you wanted? To be able to stand and gloat? How much you must enjoy knowing how easily you could destroy me! Was that why you took me to bed, Nash, because you felt you owned me?'

Nash could see the tears of fury and shame in her eyes and he closed his own, mentally cursing the appalling timing of his solicitor's innocent disclosures.

Whatever he tried to say now Faith was going to misinterpret it, and she was certainly in no mood to listen to what he *had* wanted to say to her. As for that new beginning he had so wanted to ask her to make...

'I wasn't the one who instigated what happened between us,' he tried to remind her, and knew that he had said the wrong thing as he saw the look on her face.

'I hate you, Nash. I *hate* you,' she told him furiously, before whirling round and running up the stairs, away from him.

CHAPTER TEN

FAITH walked tensely across the hallway. Robert should be arriving soon. He had telephoned her the previous evening to say that he was going to make a flying visit to see her.

'Just to touch base, really,' he had told her, adding ruefully, 'Unfortunately there won't be time for anything else.'

'How is your cousin?' Faith had asked him.

'He's fine,' Robert had responded. 'He's nearly ninety, and he's determined to make it to his centenary.'

He had had to ring off to take another call before Faith could say any more.

What was she going to tell him about the problems she could see confronting them with the conversion of Hatton? She desperately wanted to be able to give him some good news, but she was becoming increasingly concerned about the suitability of Hatton for the Foundation's purposes.

The success of this project was so important to Robert, and Faith wanted it to succeed for his sake. Perhaps another more experienced architect might be able to see an answer that was hidden from her?

As she heard a car pulling up outside she hurried

towards the front door, pausing as the sunlight caught the gold of her wedding ring.

That was something else she was going to have to tell Robert. But tell him what? Certainly not that she was trapped in a marriage that was no marriage at all and never would be, nor that she prayed passionately at night in bed—the bed she slept in alone—that she had been wrong about that spark of life she had felt ignite when she and Nash had made love. Made *love*! Who was she kidding? *She* might have thought they were making love, but what Nash had been doing was collecting an interest payment on his investment.

They had barely spoken to one another since her outburst on discovering the hidden role he had played in her life. Or rather she had made it virtually impossible for Nash to speak to her, either by avoiding him or simply walking away from him when he did try to approach her.

Only this morning he had walked into the kitchen whilst she was there, and she had seen from the look on his face that he fully intended to make her listen to him. She, though, had been equally determined not to do so, and as she had stormed past him he had taken hold of her arm—not in a painful grip, exactly, but there had been enough force there to ignite her own still smouldering fury.

Fortunately for her Mrs Jenson had arrived before Nash could say anything, giving her the opportunity to escape. But Faith had seen the look in his eyes as she had done so, and she knew she was pushing his self-control into its danger zone.

But why should she care?

The sunlight glinting on her wedding ring as she opened the door for Robert reminded her that she had still not found her missing engagement ring.

'Mmm…it's good to breathe clean air instead of city fume-choked stuff,' Robert commented appreciatively as he followed her into Philip's study.

The look he was giving her was even more appreciative, Faith recognised as he smiled at her.

'How are the plans coming along?' Robert asked her eagerly.

Faith paused, going over to the desk instead of closing the study door as she had been about to do.

'I'm having rather a few problems,' she admitted. 'The kitchen…'

She lifted her hand to show Robert the kitchen area on the plans on the desk, and went silent as she saw he was looking at her wedding ring.

'Nash and I are married,' she told him uncomfortably. 'It was… We didn't… I don't…'

Her voice trailed away as she saw how shocked Robert was.

'I knew the two of you had a…history,' he responded manfully, 'but I didn't…'

He shook his head whilst Faith watched him with a mixture of anxiety and guilt. There had been nothing serious between them, and she had no reason to feel guilty, but nevertheless she was aware that her news wasn't something he had expected or wanted to hear.

To her relief he immediately rallied and told her ruefully, 'When I asked you to use your influence to persuade Nash to finalise the Foundation's acquisition of Hatton I didn't expect you to go to *those* lengths, you know!'

Gratitude towards him for the way he was trying to ease the situation for her filled Faith, but outside in the hallway, where he had been on his way to speak to Robert, Nash froze.

His immediate instinctive interpretation of Robert's comment filled him with bitter anger. Faith had used him—used his love for her for her own ends.

Faith gave Robert a shaky smile as she shook her head.

'I wish I *could* do something to help you,' she admitted. 'You've been so kind to me, Robert.'

To her chagrin her eyes filled with tears, and she knew that Robert had seen them.

'Hey, what's all this?' he demanded softly, closing the space between them and giving her a comforting hug.

Faith had her back to the door and her face buried against Robert's shoulder, so she didn't see Nash stride into the study. But Robert did, immediately releasing her as he said self-consciously, 'Oh, Nash. I understand that congratulations are in order. Faith has just been telling me your good news.'

'So I can see,' Nash agreed curtly, giving Faith a

look of icy contempt before turning away from her
to tell Robert, 'Perhaps once you've finished ''con-
gratulating'' her you could spare *me* five minutes?
There's something I want to discuss with you.'

Faith saw Robert drive away from her bedroom window. She had gone there to leave the two men to
their discussions following Nash's arrival in the
study.

Her face burned with a mixture of anger and resentment.

Nash had had no right to look at her the way he
had, with that...that contempt, that almost murder-
ous loathing. It had been obvious from Robert's reaction that he'd felt he was confronting a savagely
jealous husband, but *she*, of course, had known better.

How much longer must she wait before knowing
whether or not she had conceived Nash's child?
How many days' grace should she give herself? She
knew there were home tests one could do, but surely
it was still too early for that?

She froze as her bedroom door crashed open and
Nash strode in.

'So Ferndown asked you to used your ''influence'' with me, did he?' he demanded without pre-
amble. 'Don't bother denying it, Faith. I overheard
the pair of you.'

'And, typically of you, Nash, you immediately
leaped to conclusions and made judgements based
on those conclusions. Does it ever occur to you that

you could possibly misjudge something? No, of course it doesn't,' Faith told him scornfully, answering her own question. 'All Robert wanted was to know what the Foundation's position was with regard to Hatton. He didn't realise... He didn't know...'

'He didn't know what, Faith? He didn't know just what lengths you'd go to...just how *dedicated* you can be? Unlike me! I have your tutors' reports, after all, and yet I still fell for it. I still let you— How many times were you prepared to have sex with me before you asked for what you wanted?'

'How *dare* you say that?' Faith choked furiously. 'I didn't...'

'You didn't what?' Nash demanded. 'You didn't go to bed with me as a calculated manoeuvre...out of self-interest and greed? If it wasn't for that, Faith, then what was it for?' he asked her with frighteningly savage softness. 'Was it for this?'

He moved as swiftly as a big cat on its prey, all raw male energy, strength and muscle as his body enveloped her, imprisoning hers with ease.

Don't touch me, she wanted to cry—but the words remained locked in her throat, just as the angry fists she wanted to beat against his chest in a frantic bid for freedom remained locked at her sides.

Was it her own anger that was paralysing her so completely? Faith wondered dizzily. Or was it Nash's unleashed male power?

'You're my wife, Faith,' she heard him saying as his mouth covered hers. 'Mine...'

His—bought and paid for! The wild ferocity of her own reaction shocked Faith, but she was totally unable to control it—just as she was totally unable to control the sharp bite of her teeth against Nash's mouth as she fought against the possession of his kiss.

But as fire met fire and the resulting conflagration was driven by the wind nothing could stand in its way to stop it.

Faith was conscious of Nash's thick curse as her teeth raked his lip. She could taste his blood on her tongue and feel the savagery of his hands as he held her, dragging her further into his body, not pushing her away, his mouth opening with shocking demand over hers.

Scarcely knowing what she was doing, Faith raked her nails down his forearm, twisting and turning as she fought to break free of him. And yet, for all her fury, somewhere deep down inside her body there was a growing sense of excitement, of arousal, of a dangerous, previously unknown instinct.

She felt as feral, as filled with conflict of needs and urges, as a she-wolf, Faith recognised breathlessly. Panting with heat and desire for the male who wanted to mate with her and yet at the same time snarling her aggression and hostility towards him as her enemy.

In Nash too she could sense the same feelings. Hostility crossed with desire was a volatile, explosive mix of emotions—a need by both of them to prove who was the stronger emotionally.

This was the dark side of the tender intimacy with which she had given herself to him before, and as she fought against him Faith knew that if she were to win and he let her go there would be an ache deep down inside her that desperately needed to be satisfied; that could only be satisfied by Nash.

Faith leaned closer to Nash, tipping back her head to expose the vulnerable softness of her throat. Her body arched back over his arm, her mouth swollen from the savagery of their angry passion.

As he looked down at her Nash could feel his muscles bunching like those of an animal, coiled to spring forward for the kill. He could see the pulse quivering in her throat, and the urge to cover it with his mouth, take it…take *her*…was so strong he could hear it roaring in his own ears.

Why *should* he act with conscience or listen to any voice pleading clemency? Hadn't Faith by her own actions put herself in a position where she didn't merit either? He could take her now, fill her with the urgent possessive heat of his body and take them both to a white-hot place that for a breath of time would taste like heaven. But then, afterwards, he would have to live with what he had done, what level he had allowed himself to be dragged down to.

Abruptly he released her.

Unsteadily Faith reached out to stop herself from falling, her eyes wide with shock and disbelief as she saw the distance Nash had put between them.

A part of him had known all along just what he

was inviting by giving in to the dark urge that had
driven him to keep Faith in his life, Nash recognised, as the red mist of his anger faded to be replaced by a sickening sense of self-loathing. Wreak-
ing vengeance on her might not have been an
obsession, but he had certainly been guilty of believing that he owed it to Philip to see that she was
never allowed to forget what she had done.

Turning on his heel, he strode towards the door.

Silently Faith watched him go. They had come so
close to the edge of an abyss. Faith shuddered in
shock as she realised how close.

What had so nearly happened between them just
now must never, ever be allowed to happen again.
She couldn't remain here now, anyway. Not even
if... Her hand touched her stomach as she made a
silent apology to the child she might be carrying for
depriving him or her of a father.

Once she was back in London she would get in
touch with Robert and tell him about her past, and
then she would start looking for a new job—abroad,
perhaps, where she could make a fresh start, where
there would be no Nash to torment and hurt her.
And no escape either from her own realisation of
just how strong her love for him was.

How she could love him still she had no idea; all
she knew was that she *did*.

Meticulously Faith looked round her room.

Yes, everything was packed—not that there had
been much to pack. Her wedding outfit and its ac-

cessories had been carefully returned to their boxes and would be left for Nash to dispose of as he pleased. If his mood yesterday was anything to go by he would probably burn them at the stake on an effigy of her, Faith decided wryly. Her work was in her case ready to be returned to Robert. There was only one task she had yet to complete.

Very carefully she removed her wedding ring and placed it in the box that held her earrings.

Nash had left the house earlier—she had no idea where he had gone, was only glad that he had. This way at least she could leave with some semblance of dignity, without breaking down and crying to him, pleading with him as she had done all those years ago.

She frowned as she started to close the small jewellery box. She still hadn't found her engagement ring. Perhaps Mrs Jenson the housekeeper might have come across it when she had been tidying up. Very slowly and carefully Faith made her way downstairs to go the kitchen.

Nash frowned grimly at the building in front of him. It was derelict now, a burden to the council who owned it, its windows broken and its grounds overgrown. It had always looked a bleak, institutionalised sort of place to him, and he had felt desperately for Faith having to live there. A children's *home*! Home was the last thing it looked like.

He had no idea why he had driven here, or what answers he had been hoping to go find. What answers, after all, were there? How *could* he love a woman who made him despise himself for doing so? At Philip's graveside he had told the older man that she had been young, misguided, and that whilst he, Nash, would never forget, he wanted to put aside the past and forgive, make a new start for Faith, for himself—and, perhaps most importantly of all, for the child they might have created. And then he had heard her conversation with Ferndown! Once again Faith had condemned herself.

The look in his eyes was as bleak as the place in front of him as he turned and walked away from it, back to his car.

'Mrs Jenson, I wonder if I could have a word with...' Shock froze Faith to the spot as she stared at the woman standing next to the housekeeper.

'Charlene,' she whispered in disbelief.

'Aunt Em said you'd turned up here,' the other woman smirked. 'What a turn-up for the books, eh? Who'd have thought it, after what you done? Bold as brass, some people are... Wait 'til it gets out in the town that there's a murderess living here...'

Faith had had enough.

'That's not true,' she denied swiftly. 'You know perfectly well that I had *nothing* to do with what happened. It was you and the rest of your little gang. You lied about me, blamed me...implicating me when *I* was trying to protect Philip.'

For a moment the horror of the past threatened to overwhelm Faith. She was still in shock from walking into Hatton's kitchen and discovering there the very person who had been responsible for the break-in, the very person who had callously threatened and frightened Philip. She flinched as the girl she had known as Charlene Jenks laughed.

'You asked for it, Miss Too-good-to-be-true, running telling tales on us, trying to get us into trouble. You deserved everything you got,' she added viciously, her eyes suddenly sharp little spikes of malice. 'I can still see your face when the police hauled you away along with the rest of us. ''Nash, don't let them take me,''' she mocked, mimicking Faith's soft voice. '''Nash, you can't believe I would ever hurt Philip...'''

'But he did believe it, and why shouldn't he have done? You made it all so easy. There you were, caught red-handed with the old fool's wallet in your hand. All we'd done was follow your instructions, we said. You were the one who planned it all. You were the one who knew he'd be in the house on his own, who knew how to get in. You just knocked on the door and told him it was you, didn't you? And he let you in. That's what we said and everyone believed us. Including your precious Nash!'

'Stop it! Stop!' Faith protested, covering her ears, her face white. 'How could you have done it? How *could* you have frightened him...hurt him like that?'

Faith's voice shook with emotion as she spoke. Outside the half-closed kitchen door Nash stood in silence, his body rigid with shock.

He had walked into the empty hallway and decided to head for the kitchen to make himself a cup of coffee, but as he had approached the doorway he had heard the women's voices coming from inside the room and he had stopped—and listened. At first his heartbeat had accelerated, pounding fast with shock. Now it had slowed down to heavy, agonised thuds of anguished despair.

Faith was innocent—just as she had claimed all along. How she must hate him now.

Inside the kitchen Charlene Jenks was still taunting Faith.

'It was easy... Until we got caught, thanks to you bursting in like that and ruining everything. Still, we made you pay for it.' She started to scowl. 'Trust you to get off with it, though. Course, we all know who was responsible for that. He must have had the hots for you even then, your precious Nash, to speak up for you the way he did. Heard all about it, we did—how he'd begged the magistrate to treat you leniently. Going to bed with you even then, was he? And you under-age? Just wait until we spread that tale around the town.'

Faith came out of the shock Charlene's revelations had given her.

'Don't you dare even think about spreading those kind of lies about Nash,' she told her passionately.

Nash had interceded for her! *Nash* was the one who had spoken up for her...saved her from being sentenced...

On the other side of the door, Nash had heard enough. Pushing it fully open, he strode into the kitchen, ignoring the housekeeper and turning to confront Charlene.

'Just *one* more word, *one* more threat, and you'll find yourself having to explain to the police,' Nash told her grimly. 'And as for you,' he told Mrs Jenson as Charlene started to back away from him, her face pallid with shock and apprehension, 'you're fired—and don't even think about asking for a reference.'

'I haven't done anything,' the older woman began to protest truculently. 'It was our Charlene that wanted to come up here. Said she'd got an old score to settle.'

Maliciously she glowered at Faith, but when Nash moved towards her Faith shook her head, saying immediately, 'No, Nash, ignore her.'

'Let me warn you,' she could hear Nash saying as he walked them towards the back door, 'I fully intend to go to the police and register a complaint against both of you.'

Faith could tell from his tone that he meant what he said, and she could see that they could too.

Her shock was wearing off now, and by the time Nash had closed the kitchen door and they were alone she had finally managed to steady her quivering limbs.

'What can I say?' Nash asked her bleakly.

'You weren't to know,' Faith responded, her voice as dry as death. 'All the evidence was against me. I was there, next to Philip, holding his wallet. They said I was the one to plan everything, that it was my idea.'

'You asked me to listen...to trust you...'

Faith looked away from him in silence.

'I should *never* have left Philip that night,' Nash castigated himself harshly. 'I *knew* how weak he had become, but my damned work...'

He said the words with such guilt and self-loathing that Faith's heart ached for him. Tentatively she lifted her hand in a gesture of comfort, and then let it fall again.

'In insisting that *you* feel guilt, Faith, what I was doing was trying to sidestep my own guilt. I needed to be able to blame you because it stopped me from blaming myself.'

'Why did you intercede for me?' Faith asked him in a low voice. She couldn't bring herself to look at him whilst she waited for his response, twisting her hands together and feeling the heavy, driven thud of her own heart.

'Why the hell do you think?' Nash asked in a gritty, emotion-laden voice. 'You must have sensed how I felt about you, Faith, and how—' He stopped, and Faith lifted her head and searched his face, her eyes huge and dark.

'I know how I felt about *you*,' she admitted shakily. 'You were kind to me, but...' She hesitated, trying carefully to pick her way safely through the minefield of self-doubt and fear that distanced her, separated her from the shining beacon of her growing hope.

'Kind!' Nash made an explosive sound. 'Kindness wasn't what I wanted to give you, Faith. What I *wanted* to give you, share with you, was...' He looked down at her and she could see the hot male glitter in his eyes. Immediately her own senses sprang into response.

'I wanted you, Faith,' Nash told her rawly. 'Wanted you in all the ways a man of my age had no right to want an under-age child.'

'I *wasn't* a child. I was fifteen,' Faith protested.

'Fifteen, sixteen—eighteen, even. It wouldn't have made any difference,' Nash told her grimly. 'You were too young, too inexperienced for what I wanted with you.'

Stunned, Faith told him fiercely, 'Sexual experience isn't everything. It isn't a barometer of how a person can really feel when...'

'I'm not talking about *sexual* experience,' Nash informed her. 'I'm talking about your experience of *life*, your right to experience life *for* yourself and *by* yourself. If I had given in to my feelings for you then, to my need for you, my *love* for you...'

He paused whilst Faith's heart leaped frantically against her chest wall at the sound of the word 'love'.

'It wouldn't just have been the law of the land I'd have been breaking if I'd given you my love then, Faith. It would have been my own moral code as well, the one Philip taught me.'

'Perhaps if Philip had made a full recovery from his stroke and been able to tell you what had happened...'

'Why should I have needed Philip to tell me?'

Nash asked her harshly. 'I should have known for *myself.*'

'Why did you pay for my education?' Faith asked him quietly. '*Was* it just because you wanted to have power over me?'

'It was what Philip wanted,' Nash told her shortly, but Faith was sure he wasn't telling her everything.

'The earrings you bought me,' she persisted, 'for my twenty-first birthday...'

'Your tutors' reports stressed how hard you'd worked. I knew you had no family,' Nash told her curtly. 'Hell, Faith, what is it you want me to say?' he demanded when she made no response. 'That I bought them because there wasn't a day when I didn't ache for you...there wasn't a *night* when I didn't wish I could forget what had happened to Philip?'

'Did you offer Hatton to the Foundation because of me?' she asked him shakily in the fraught silence that followed his passionate outburst.

Nash shook his head. 'Not consciously. But...'

'But?' Faith pressed.

'The truth sits between us, Faith. I can never forgive myself.'

'In this instance surely any forgiveness is within *my* gift rather than yours?' Faith pointed out wryly.

But although she held on to her breath, and her hope, Nash made no attempt to reach for the ladder she had thrown him to cross the gulf between them.

'The best thing we can hope for now is that there isn't going to be a child,' he told her heavily. 'We should be able to end our marriage reasonably easily.'

Desperately Faith demanded, 'And what if I don't want to end it?'

Nash sighed and walked over to her.

'Do you think I haven't guessed what you really want?' he asked her tautly.

Faith held her breath again, waiting to hear him tell her that no matter how much she still loved him he could not return her feelings. But to her bemusement he continued harshly, 'I have to set you free to make your own life, Faith.'

What on earth was Nash saying? He must surely know that *he* was all she wanted. This must be his way of being tactful, of saving her pride. But her pride was the last thing she cared about now. And yet as Nash walked towards the kitchen door and away from her, for some reason she didn't ask him the one question that could potentially have kept him with her. What if, as she suspected, she *was* pregnant? Would he still want to end their marriage then?

Outside in the garden Nash stared unseeingly into the distance. It was too late for him to regret his behaviour now, but not too late for him to suffer the reality of his own shame. All those years ago he hadn't believed her because he had been afraid of doing so, afraid of his love for her and what it might do to them both. It had been easier to tell himself that she wasn't worthy of his love when the truth was that he hadn't been worthy of hers!

*   *   *

There was nothing for her here at Hatton now, Faith acknowledged as she headed for her bedroom. She ought to be feeling glad, triumphant, proud that Nash had finally accepted her innocence, and not... Not what? Not aching with love and need for him, not wishing that he still loved her?

Automatically she touched her wedding ring, and then frowned as she suddenly remembered that she *had* been wearing her engagement ring on the night of the storm, when she had fled to the sanctuary of Nash's room and Nash's bed...

Emotional pain did the most extraordinary things to a human being, Nash acknowledged as he made his way towards his bedroom and contemplated the wasteland his life had now become.

As he opened the door he saw that Faith was sitting on his bed, her face turned slightly away from him. He could see a single tear glisteningly rolling over her cheek as she studied the rings on her hand.

'What are you crying for?' he asked her harshly.

Faith started as she saw him. She had found her ring underneath Nash's bed, where it must have rolled.

'For what might have been,' she told Nash sadly and honestly. 'If...'

'If what?' Nash prompted her.

'If you hadn't stopped loving me, Nash,' she told him steadily.

'*Stopped* loving you?' Nash exhaled sharply. 'I have *never* stopped loving you, Faith,' he told her thickly. 'I couldn't—no matter how many times I wished to God that I could.'

'But you hated me as well.'

'I hated my own inability to control my love for you,' Nash corrected her. 'It's ironic, I suppose, that after years of fighting against myself, when I finally managed to make my peace with myself and confess to Philip that not even the loyalty I owe him could stop me from loving you, I should discover that *I* was the one who was guilty of the real sin.'

Faith started to frown.

'I don't understand—' she began, but Nash stopped her.

'The night of the storm...when you...when we... I decided then that it was time to lay the past to rest. I went to Philip's grave...'

The night of the storm! Suddenly Faith knew what she had to do. She must be the embodiment of her own name. She must have courage and conviction.

Slowly she stood up and walked over to where Nash was standing. When she reached him she said softly, 'The night of the storm? When I kissed you like this...?'

And she put her arms round him and stretched up to reach his mouth, slowly and very deliberately caressing it with all the power and determination of a woman in love.

'Faith...' Nash protested on a low groan. 'You mustn't...'

'Why not?' she whispered boldly, feathering the

words tormentingly against his aching mouth. 'I'm your wife and you're my husband...my love...the father of my child...'

As he opened his mouth to protest she closed her own over it, kissing him with passion and love.

He moved, lifting his hands to her arms, and for a moment she thought he was going to push her away. But then his hands slid over her arms and he was drawing her closer, taking control of the kiss from her. Tenderly she yielded it to him.

'Tell me that you love me,' he demanded thickly in between kisses.

'Not until *you've* told me,' Faith responded, smiling.

Abruptly Nash released her, and for a moment she thought she had got it wrong, overplayed her hand... And then he was entwining his fingers with hers as he commanded, 'Come with me. I want to show you something.'

By the time they reached the gazebo at the end of the walkway Faith was almost out of breath. It was a perfect summer evening, balmily soft, scented with roses and lavender.

'The first time I stood here and saw you,' Nash told her softly, 'I knew how much I loved you, how much I would always love you—and I do, Faith.'

'Tell me again how you felt that first time you saw me,' she urged him.

'Tell you?' Nash questioned. 'I've got a much better idea. Why don't I show you instead?'

'Out here in the garden?' Faith whispered, semi-shocked but more excited.

'Out here in the garden,' Nash agreed, and he drew her to him and began to kiss and caress her.

EPILOGUE

'PHILIPPA. It's such a pretty name.'

Faith smiled warmly at Robert Ferndown's fiancée Lucy as both Robert and Lucy cooed over baby Philippa where she lay snugly in her father's arms.

She was three months old and today she was being christened, at the same church where Faith and Nash had been married.

They had asked Robert and Lucy to be godparents—a strong bond of friendship had begun to develop between the four of them, and Faith was looking forward to attending their marriage later in the year.

'I do so envy you Hatton,' Lucy had told Faith the first time Robert had introduced her to them.

Faith had smiled.

'It *is* a lovely house,' she had agreed serenely, turning away from the other girl to watch Nash.

She had still been pregnant with Philippa then. It had been Christmas, and for their first Christmas together Nash had sent away the army of builders who had taken over Hatton after he had decided that instead of giving the house to the Foundation he and Faith should make it their family home.

'We shall need an awful lot of these,' Faith had

laughed, patting her bulge when he had told her, 'to fill it!'

'So...?' he had teased back, lifting one eyebrow.

'Robert will be disappointed for the Foundation,' she had warned him.

'I've got something else in mind for Robert,' Nash had informed her.

'Oh? What?' she had asked, staring at him in bemusement when he told her.

'The old children's home where I...? But...'

'I've made enquiries and the council is willing to sell it to me. The house can be demolished and a new one built—a proper home—not an institution.'

'And you'd do that and give it to Robert? Oh, Nash...'

'Don't you dare say "Oh, Nash" to me like that in your condition,' he had warned her. 'You temptress...'

Philippa stirred in her father's arms. They had named her for Philip, a loving tribute to him.

'If you keep on gazing adoringly at her like that I'm going to get jealous,' Faith warned Nash untruthfully as she left Lucy to slip her arm through her husband's.

'Wait until tonight,' Nash whispered to her as they walked towards the church. 'And then I'll show you just how little cause you have to feel neglected or jealous. You will always be first in my life and in my heart, my darling, darling Faith.'

Pick up a Harlequin Presents® novel and enter a world of spine-tingling passion and provocative, tantalizing romance!

Join us in December for two sexy Italian heroes from two of your favorite authors:

RAFAELLO'S MISTRESS
by Lynne Graham
#2217

THE ITALIAN'S RUNAWAY BRIDE
by Jacqueline Baird
#2219

HARLEQUIN *Presents*

The world's bestselling romance series.
Seduction and passion guaranteed.

Available wherever Harlequin books are sold.

Visit us at www.eHarlequin.com
HPITAL

CALL THE ONES YOU LOVE OVER THE HOLIDAYS!

Save $25 off future book purchases when you buy any four Harlequin® or Silhouette® books in October, November and December 2001,

PLUS

receive a phone card good for 15 minutes of long-distance calls to anyone you want in North America!

WHAT AN INCREDIBLE DEAL!

Just fill out this form and attach 4 proofs of purchase (cash register receipts) from October, November and December 2001 books, and Harlequin Books will send you a coupon booklet worth a total savings of $25 off future purchases of Harlequin® and Silhouette® books, AND a 15-minute phone card to call the ones you love, anywhere in North America.

Please send this form, along with your cash register receipts as proofs of purchase, to:
In the USA: Harlequin Books, P.O. Box 9057, Buffalo, NY 14269-9057
In Canada: Harlequin Books, P.O. Box 622, Fort Erie, Ontario L2A 5X3
Cash register receipts must be dated no later than December 31, 2001.
Limit of 1 coupon booklet and phone card per household.
Please allow 4-6 weeks for delivery.

I accept your offer! Enclosed are 4 proofs of purchase. Please send me my coupon booklet and a 15-minute phone card:

Name: _____

Address: _____ City: _____

State/Prov.: _____ Zip/Postal Code: _____

Account Number (if available): _____

097 KJB DAGL
PHQ4013

HARLEQUIN *Presents*

The world's
bestselling romance series.
Seduction and passion
guaranteed!

Pick up a Harlequin Presents® novel and you
will enter a world of spine-tingling passion
and provocative, tantalizing romance!

Join us next month for an exciting selection
of titles from all your favorite authors,
each one part of a miniseries:

Red Hot Revenge
THE MARRIAGE DEMAND
by **Penny Jordan**
#2211

The Australians
FUGITIVE BRIDE
by **Miranda Lee**
#2212

Latin Lovers
A SPANISH AFFAIR
by **Helen Brooks**
#2213

9 to 5
THE BOSS'S VIRGIN
by **Charlotte Lamb**
#2214

Christmas
THE MISTRESS DEAL
by **Sandra Field**
#2215

Greek Tycoons
THE KYRIAKIS BABY
by **Sara Wood**
#2216

On sale November
Available wherever Harlequin books are sold.